DAREDEVILS

By

Joy Lynn Goddard

© 2003 by Joy Lynn Goddard. All rights reserved.

No part of this book may be reproduced, stored in a retrieval system, or transmitted by any means, electronic, mechanical, photocopying, recording, or otherwise, without written permission from the author.

ISBN: 1-4107-2763-7 (e-book)
ISBN: 1-4107-2764-5 (Paperback)

This book is printed on acid free paper.

My gratitude goes to Burl Levine, my editor and friend, and Mary Sephton, an awesome goalie . . .

1stBooks - rev. 04/29/03

For Dan, Jeff, and Rob

And in memory of Jackie . . .

CHAPTER 1
DREAMER

The dressing room was hot and smelled of wet boots and sweaty bodies and the hot chocolate with marshmallows served from Mr. Murphy's concession stand. Lizzie's chest pads were already clammy although she hadn't been on the ice yet. She brushed her blonde hair away from her face and tied it into a ponytail, then pulled on a helmet.

Sitting between Trevor and Sean on the long wooden bench, the only opening, Lizzie began to tighten her skate laces. The boys ignored her, as they usually did, especially Trevor, and carried on a conversation over her head.

"Did you see Number 9 on the Wolves?" Trevor's eyes bugged out. "He's humongous."

"Don't let that scare you," Sean said. "You're faster and mean. We're gonna destroy the Wolves."

Trevor shot Lizzie a meaningful look. "Not with *her* in net."

With a heavy sigh, she stood up and turned her back to the boys. There wasn't time to fight with them because the game was about to begin, and besides, Lizzie wanted to use every bit of energy on the ice. She clumped over the wooden floorboards to the door. The whistle blew and the Zamboni machine droned to a stop. It was time to warm up.

As she slid onto the ice in front of hundreds of spectators, her stomach was in knots. She hadn't touched a drop of the green, smelly tea that her mother had sent to the rink to settle Lizzie's stomach, because none of the other players drank tea before a big game, and she usually felt better once her mind was on the net.

The play began as the puck hit the ice at centre. With every muscle tensed, Lizzie hunched in the net, ready. The Wolves raced towards her. They were bigger than the Tigers, Lizzie's team, and they were also better at handling the puck. Lizzie realized this from the first few minutes of play. Number 9 forced the puck away from the Tigers' Number 4 and skidded in front of the net. Lizzie's heart jumped. Loud cries with feet stomping came from the crowds in the stands. As the puck smashed towards Lizzie, she deflected it with an arm.

The crowd went wild. She felt her mother's eyes from the stands, glued to every move. Her mother's boyfriend, Pete, would be watching the Tigers play too, and he'd be cheering for her at the top of his lungs. Sometimes being shot at was worth all the trouble.

It wasn't long before Number 9 was swooping towards her again. The Tigers' defence, Number 8, tried to keep the puck away by passing it to Sean, Number 7. Sean fumbled and fell, knocking over a Wolves' player. Nothing could stop Number 9. He darted through a mass of Wolves and shot. Lizzie threw her body at the flying puck, but it was a split second too late and the puck slammed into the net.

She stared hard at the ice for what seemed like forever, afraid to look at any of the other Tigers. When she finally looked up, almost everyone was giving her a dirty look, especially Trevor. The only one ignoring her was Alex, who was busy skating around in circles at the blueline.

As the horn signaled the end of the third period, the Wolves had beaten the Tigers 4-1. In the dressing room afterwards, no one said a word for the longest time. The coach, Mr. Powers, bustled into the room, telling the players that they'd played a good game, but Lizzie tuned him out. As she pulled off her helmet, her arms felt like lead. All she could think about was getting her skates off and going home. She dragged her equipment bag out the door and into the waiting area.

She found her mother with Pete near the concession bar talking to Mr. Murphy, the proprietor. "Great game, Lizzie." Her mother was all smiles as she handed her a steaming cup of hot chocolate.

"You kept me on the edge of my seat," Pete said, his eyes wide.

Lizzie hung her head. "But we lost."

"Technically, yes," Pete nodded, and went on, "but you're always a winner when you try your best, and you were really working hard out there." He always made her feel better. He wasn't anything like his daughter, Tara, who made Lizzie feel miserable every chance she got.

In the Lockyer family, there were just two people, Lizzie and her mother, Laura. Lizzie's father had died when she was just a baby, and her mother had never remarried. Laura had dated a few times, but no one special, until Pete. He and his daughter came over to the house often, especially on weekends, and Lizzie liked Pete's company, but she wasn't too crazy about his daughter's. Tara took over the house. She was always hogging the phone or computer or playing a CD so loudly that nobody could concentrate on anything else. Laura said that Tara was just being a normal teenager, but Lizzie didn't think that Tara was normal at all.

Tara was sitting cross-legged on the living room floor with the CD player and television blaring at the same time as Lizzie, Laura and Pete came home after the game. Carefully applying blue polish to her fingernails, she didn't look up.

Joy Lynn Goddard

"Hi sweetie," Pete said. "Watch that blue stuff doesn't get on the carpet."

"Okay."

"Lizzie played a great game," Pete said.

"Hmm, that's nice." Tara brought her nails to her lips and blew on them gently. She couldn't care less about the game, Lizzie thought. She'd said about a hundred times that Lizzie was "a big freak" for being the only girl on a boys' team. "There's no more popcorn," Tara grumbled.

"There's some in the cupboard above the fridge," Laura said, turning to the kitchen. "I'll make you some." She was always ready to jump whenever Tara so much as made a peep about anything, and this got on Lizzie's nerves.

The smell of hot, buttery popcorn filled the house. Lizzie took a bowl and wandered into the family room, away from the others. When she wanted to be alone, it wasn't hard; her house was large with lots of rooms. It was much better than the cramped, one-bedroom apartment across the city where she and her mother had lived for many years. The house was a little rundown and drafty, and it creaked and rattled with scary sounds in the middle of the night, but Lizzie didn't mind.

She also didn't mind that the basement was off limits because a tenant lived there. His name was Tom, a university student who helped pay the rent. Sometimes he talked to Lizzie about computers and stuff, but most of the time he kept to himself, studying or cooking meals with spicy aromas that drifted up through the vents into Lizzie's bedroom.

She picked up the remote control and started flipping channels. A hockey game was madly in progress on the sports channel. She stopped to watch but couldn't concentrate. In her mind she was in the net with puck after puck flying at her. She dreamed of blocking every single puck and leading the Tigers to victory. The Tigers would win the championship game, and Lizzie would be presented with the MVG award at the year-end banquet.

The phone rang, breaking into her dreams. When she picked it up she found dead silence at the other end.

Joy Lynn Goddard

She cried into the receiver, "Hello, hello?" There was a clunk at the other end. As soon as she hung up, the phone rang again.

"Why don't you play with girls and leave us guys alone," the caller growled. He sounded familiar. Trevor.

"Ya, get your own team," another voice joined in, "or go play with your Barbie dolls." It was Sean, Trevor's best friend.

Lizzie swallowed hard. She tried to say something, but the words stuck in her throat like peanut butter. She wanted to say that she'd gladly play on a girls' team if there were any good teams in Northview, but there weren't any, and that's why she was stuck playing on the boys' team. The phone went dead again.

When it rang a third time, she was more than ready to get things off her chest. "If it weren't for me, you guys would be in last place," she shrieked.

There was silence at the other end of the phone. It was followed by a hesitant, "Lizzie, is that you?" The voice was small and quiet. It was vaguely familiar. "Um, this is Alex, you know, Alex Fabiano."

"Oh, hi," Lizzie said with an embarrassed laugh. "I thought it was, um, Sean or Trevor. I didn't mean to yell at you."

"That's okay. I was just phoning because . . ." He cleared his throat. "Well, you looked kinda bad after we lost. It wasn't your fault. Number 9 was pretty gruesome. You played a good game."

"Oh." Lizzie racked her brains but couldn't think of anything else to say. This was the first time Alex had called her, and he wasn't really her friend. He was kind of a loner at school.

"Well, that's all I wanted to say," he said. "See you Monday."

Before she could answer, the phone went dead again.

CHAPTER 2
OF FURRY CREATURES GREAT AND SMALL

The smell of bacon drifted into Lizzie's room Monday morning as she awoke hungry, her stomach growling under the thick quilt that covered her bed. It was still dark outside although the digital clock on the night stand read 7:15 a.m. The wind was howling and lashing snow pellets against the small window in the bedroom, and Lizzie hoped school would be closed because of the bad weather. She turned on the radio beside her bed to hear a weather report and snuggled deeper under the covers.

At the end of some whiney country music, the announcer's mellow voice warned: "Careful if you're driving today. High winds and ice pellets have made the highways pretty slick. And kids, don't get back into bed." He chuckled. "Schools are still open. Buses will be running late, though."

Disgusted, Lizzie threw off the covers and hurried across the cold hardwood floor to the bathroom. Her mother was rushing from her bedroom, dressed in her favourite outfit, a black skirt, a white blouse and a rose blazer. She was combing her hair with one hand and putting on a black shoe with the other. Lizzie assumed that her mother had been called to supply teach. She got about three calls a week, and with trying to complete her degree and teaching piano, she often ran around like a crazy woman.

Lizzie groaned, "Thought we'd get a day off."

"No such luck," her mother said. "Get a move on if you want a ride. I'm teaching across town today, so I've got to start early."

"That's okay, I'll walk. It's not far." Lizzie didn't want to get to school too early and look too keen.

As the bell rang, a steady stream of kids wearing a rainbow of coats, hats and snow pants trudged through the hallways and into the classrooms.

Lizzie kicked off her boots at the back of the classroom, hung her coat on the hook and plunked her books on the desk as she took her seat next to Emily. The other kids in her group hadn't arrived yet.

Joy Lynn Goddard

"Too bad about school, eh?" Lizzie let out a heavy sigh.

"Hmm, what's that?" Emily had her nose in a book about earthquakes.

"School, you know. Snow. Ice. We should've had a day off."

"A little grumpy, aren't you?" Emily asked, "Let me guess, you had a bad weekend letting in too many goals. Right? You always come to school in a bad mood after that happens."

Deep down Lizzie knew Emily was right. Emily was always right, and it really bugged Lizzie. But Emily was the only real friend Lizzie had in class, even if they didn't have much in common. At least Emily wasn't all stupid about boys yet like most of the other girls.

The bell rang again, and the principal's deep, warm voice came over the P.A. "Good morning, students and teachers. Please stand for our National Anthem."

The kids stood at attention while "O Canada" was broadcast throughout the room. No one sang, except Mary who took singing lessons, and Ms. Borlino, the teacher, who was often humming or singing when she wasn't teaching a lesson or mad at a kid. With her long dark hair flowing down her back, Ms. Borlino stood as straight as the wooden pointer she used to point to the work on the board, and she sung with all her heart. She was wearing black pants and a snow-white sweater. Her gold necklace matched her earrings. Lizzie examined her teacher from head to foot, planning to tell Laura later every detail about Ms. Borlino's clothing and accessories. All the girls told their mothers what Ms. Borlino wore each day, especially the day she wore a short leather skirt to school and got in a whole lot of trouble from the principal, Mr. Porcellato. He said (according to Lisa, who swears she accidentally heard the conversation between Mr. Porcellato and Ms. Borlino) that Ms. Borlino was not dressed appropriately for a school environment and that she should go home and change.

"Good morning, everyone." Ms. Borlino scanned the classroom and smiled. "How was the weekend?"

"Good. Fine. Awful," everyone said at once.

Joy Lynn Goddard

"I couldn't get my homework done, Ms. Borlino," Ricky said. "I had to go to my Nonna's house and she kept me busy all weekend."

"Is that so?"

"I got mine done," Lisa said. "My mom made me."

"Good for her."

The classroom door opened and Adam walked in with a large box-shaped item, which was draped in a brown towel. "Sorry I'm late, Ms. Borlino," he said. "I had to bring my hamster to school. She had babies and I wanted to show everybody." He placed the cage on a nearby table and slipped off the towel.

"It was really cool," Adam said. "When I went to bed on Saturday night there were just two teddy bear hamsters. On Sunday morning there were eleven. Teddy had nine babies!"

All the kids leaned forward in their desks, straining to get a better look at the hamsters. The mother hamster huddled in the corner of the wire cage with her babies partially hidden under her gray fur. The father hamster was drinking from the spout of a glass bottle that was hanging on the cage.

"The babies don't have any fur." Adam's eyes were wide. "And they're so tiny."

"Hmm, interesting," Ms. Borlino said. "We'll all get a chance to look at the hamsters in a minute. Just stay in your seats for now."

Ms. Borlino had just finished talking when someone jumped up from the corner of the room and darted over to the cage. It was Alex. He was always out of his desk, Lizzie thought, even when the teacher had just finished telling all the students to stay in their seats. It didn't seem to matter.

His hands on the cage, Alex hunkered down to peer inside. The baby hamsters were wriggling away from their mother, each small, gray-pink body the size of an unshelled peanut. "Wow."

"Alex." Ms. Borlino was firm. "Sit down now and I'll let you come up with your group later."

Alex got up slowly and shuffled back to his desk.

Lisa leaned over to Mary and whispered, "Goon."

Mary rolled her eyes in agreement.

Joy Lynn Goddard

Lizzie ripped a piece of paper from her notebook and scribbled a few words for Emily to read:

Alex phoned me.

Yuck. Emily wrote back. *When?*

Friday night, after the game. I didn't know what to say.

What did he want? Emily asked.

He said I played a good game.

I think . . . Lizzie didn't get a chance to read the rest of Emily's note because her teacher snatched it out of her hands and tossed it into the garbage can.

Ms. Borlino brought out a large chart with several pictures of adult couples. There was one of a man and a woman kissing and another of a man and a woman holding hands, the woman pregnant.

"I'm glad you brought in the baby hamsters, Adam," Ms. Borlino said. "It ties in nicely with our Family Life Program."

The mere mention of The Family Life Program brought the entire class to attention.

Lisa gave Mary a look and shot a hand into the air. "I know about the sperm and the egg and everything, but I don't know how the sperm . . ."

"I'll answer all your questions after you've heard some of the facts," Ms. Borlino said quickly, her cheeks turning pink.

At the back of the room, Willy, Sean and Trevor started fooling around. "I already know about this stuff," Trevor said, looking smug. "We took some of it last year, and my brother told me the rest." He snickered, and some boys began to laugh. Trevor was nothing but a big know-it-all. And if he didn't know something – which was obvious when he flunked his science test – he'd blame the teacher.

Ms. Borlino took in a deep breath and let it out slowly. "Yes, Trevor, I'm sure you know something about sexuality, but I'm sure you don't know all the facts. Pay attention."

She flipped over a page on the chart and displayed a large drawing of the female reproductive system. "Now this is the uterus," she said, pointing with the wooden pointer to the diagram. "This is where the

Joy Lynn Goddard

baby grows once fertilization has taken place. Does anyone know what the tubes leading to the uterus are called?"

"Fallopian tubes." Emily sat up straight-faced and shoved her glasses back on her nose. "The egg travels from the ovaries into the Fallopian tubes." Emily knew an awful lot about science. She'd devoured most of the science books in the school library. She was going to be a doctor when she grew up, but not just an ordinary family doctor like her mother was – Emily wanted to cure cancer.

"Good for you." Ms. Borlino was all smiles. "And what happens when an egg cell meets a sperm cell in the Fallopian tube? I want the correct term."

The class fell silent. Lizzie prayed the teacher wouldn't call on her, but after looking from face to face throughout the room, Ms. Borlino fixed her eyes on Lizzie. "Lizzie?"

Lizzie lowered her eyes to the top of her desk – where somebody had scratched: *I hate school* – and ran her fingers over the letters, thinking hard. "Fertilizer," she blurted.

As the class howled, heat steadily rose from her chest to her neck and into her face. She probably looked like a bright red pimple, she thought, scrunching down in her seat and wishing madly that the floor would open up and swallow her. She never wanted to set foot in St. Mark's School again.

The teacher held up her hands to quiet the class. "I'm sure that you mean fertilization, Lizzie. Right?"

Lizzie nodded, barely looking up at the teacher. She hid her face as much as she could with her long blonde hair, a trick she'd learned in Grade One, after discovering that she had more freckles on her nose than any kid in her class.

There was a knock at the door and the class fell silent. While Ms. Borlino was talking to the school secretary, Emily leaned over and tapped Lizzie on the shoulder, her eyes flitting to the note being passed from kid to kid throughout the classroom. The note landed on Lizzie's desk. Just one word was scribbled on it: *Poophead.* It had to be from Trevor, Lizzie thought, eyeballing him from out of the corner of her

Joy Lynn Goddard

eye; he was the only one in the class with a big smirk on his face.

The attention suddenly shifted from Lizzie to Ms. Borlino as the teacher walked over to a cupboard in the back of the classroom and brought out a large plastic uterus and displayed it in front of the class. Inside was a pink doll, the size of a fist. "This is the size of the baby at . . ."

A piercing cry cut off her words.

"Oh, no!" Adam jumped out of his desk and ran to the hamster cage. "The daddy's gone. Somebody opened the cage! You!" He glared at Alex.

Alex shook his head. "No, I didn't – honestly. At least, I don't think I did." He stared blankly. "I was just looking at them." In a flash he was out of his seat, looking for the hamster under the table where the cage had been placed. Some of the girls started screaming like a bunch of hyenas and Lisa scrambled up on top of her desk. "I can't stand rodents," she cried, crouching and trembling. "They crawl up your legs and everything."

DAREDEVILS

"That's crazy." Emily shot Lisa a look of disgust. "People have this misconception about rodents and snakes. They don't crawl up your legs."

"Oh, right." Lisa stuck out her chin. "You know it all."

"I'm not going to take a chance," Mary wailed, jumping up on the desk next to Lisa's.

"Rodents are afraid of people," Emily said, planting her hands on her hips. "They try to get away from people, so they're not going to crawl up your legs, Lisa."

All the boys were crawling on the floor, looking for the hamster. Willy and Ricky searched the back cupboards after Willy said he'd seen Adam's hamster scurry into one. Emily went to the back of the room to the long row of boots under the coat hooks and she started looking inside each boot. Trevor was under Ms. Borlino's desk when the bell rang. The search for Adam's hamster was quickly abandoned, and the kids made a mad dash to the back of the room to get ready for recess.

Joy Lynn Goddard

Alex took a small saucer of food pellets from the cage and then walked over to Adam. "Let's put this food on the floor," he said. "Maybe the hamster will get hungry and come out to eat."

"It's gone." Adam fought back tears, his lips quivering. "I just know it."

CHAPTER 3

OF RUDOLPH'S NOSE AND ICY TOES

The Tigers shot out onto the ice one after the other and stretched across the blueline to wait for the whistle. Lizzie hunched down in the net, her stick out front, her skates angled, ready and watching as each player advanced to shoot the puck at her.

One after the other they skated. First there was Michael, then Sean and Alex. Each player moved the puck deftly and flung it at Lizzie. This drill always tired her the most, and she was already tired. She had rushed home after school, had finished two pages of math, had gobbled up hamburgers for dinner and had arrived at the rink at 6:30 p.m.

"Watch your peripheral," Coach Powers shouted at her from the boards as another Tiger shot. This time the puck flew close to her face and Lizzie jerked back. "Don't be afraid of the puck," Coach Powers' hands flew up. "Get right in there, Liz. Be aggressive. Like a Tiger."

The next puck slammed into Lizzie's chest pads and sent her flying; she landed with a thud on the ice. She got up as fast as she could, despite her heavy padding. She felt like she was wading in a pool with all her clothes on, like the time she'd accidentally fallen into the city pool last summer.

Back in the dressing room later, the Tigers sat on the bench listening to Coach Powers.

"Pretty good out there today," he said. "Bet we're going to make the playoffs in Niagara Falls. But that's not 'til March. And we still have the Wolves to play again."

Lizzie's stomach flip-flopped as she thought of the Wolves, especially Number 9, his humongous body racing towards her and slapping the puck with his stick.

"Next time we'll beat 'em," Sean said, shaking his fists, and the Tigers roared. Stuffing her mask and pads in her equipment bag, Lizzie overheard Trevor whisper to Sean, "They'll never see us. Not with those bushes. We'll just crawl behind 'em, and hop over when the coast is clear, then . . ."

Lizzie stared.

"Butt out," Trevor said.

"I didn't say a word," Lizzie shot back, wiping her skate blade.

"No, but your big ears were listening," Sean said.

"I couldn't help . . ." From out of the corner of her eye, she caught Alex looking in her direction. Everyone else was busy laughing, talking and getting ready for home.

"You'd be too chicken anyway," Sean hissed. He tucked his hands under his armpits and flapped his elbows like wings on a chicken. "Cluck, cluck."

"She's scared of a little bitty puck," Trevor mocked. "She's gotta be scared of *The Plan*."

Lizzie stiffened. "What plan? I'm not scared of a thing."

"Prove it, daredevil." Sean said.

It was cloudy and dark with wind whistling through tall, bare trees as Sean and Trevor led Lizzie from the arena on Exhibition Road up Park Avenue.

Joy Lynn Goddard

Her equipment bag was too heavy to drag along so Lizzie had left it in a locker in the arena.

From Park Avenue, Sean, Trevor and Lizzie headed up Greenway Drive, along the string of well-lit, old Victorian houses. Among them was a yellow brick house, set back from bushes lining the street by a long driveway. Thousands of Christmas lights twinkled from a display on the front lawn.

Lizzie leaned on the cast-iron fence in front of the property and stared in awe. There was Santa Claus in his sleigh, holding the reins of his eight reindeer, led by the shiny red burst of light from Rudolph's nose. There were many elves dressed in green with red hats and boots, poised in various stages of work on dolls and trains and trucks and sleds. Just inside the gate was a stone monument which read: *This Christmas display is a memorial to our son, John Gallina, who died in a car accident in 1974.*

"All you have to do, Lizzie," Trevor said, pulling his hat down on his head and huddling into the wind, "is grab Rudolph's nose. Just stay down as much as you can once inside the gate. Hide behind the display. And make it fast. It's colder than the Arctic out here."

"What a dumb plan," Lizzie cried. "I'm gonna get caught. The place is lit up like a house on fire."

Sean turned to Trevor. "Told ya. She's chicken."

As Lizzie glanced over her shoulder to the deserted street, a dark shadow appeared and slid behind the bushes at the side of the house. It's just my imagination, she thought, swallowing the huge lump in her throat. There was no one in the bushes or in the yellow brick house. There was no car in the driveway, and the house was dark and silent.

Afraid she'd chicken out, Lizzie hurriedly flung herself over the bushes and hunkered down on the Gallinas' property. The boys landed behind her. Crouching low, the three children clumped through the snow and hid behind some elves. Rudolph was suspended from a large wooden platform, with a ladder making the reindeer accessible. Slowly and carefully, Lizzie climbed the ladder to the platform while the boys waited below.

Her knees felt weak. She wasn't crazy about heights. She stretched a gloved hand towards Rudolph's beaming red nose and was about to unscrew it from its socket, when she suddenly drew her hand back. She couldn't do it. She'd never stolen anything in her whole life – except for that time she'd taken a bite out of a cinnamon bun in the bakery before buying it. Her mother had marched her over to the cashier and announced what Lizzie had done and then had made her pay for the bun out of her allowance. Lizzie had been mortified.

"If you gotta have his nose, you steal it," Lizzie peered over the edge of the platform and hollered through the wind at the boys below. "This is creepy."

Reaching the last rung of the ladder, she heard a voice from the bushes cry, "Quick, a car's coming."

Looking over her shoulder, her mouth fell open. There was Alex, crouched between two snow-covered shrubs. "Come on." He waved her forward. "This way."

A car horn blasted as Alex led Lizzie through an opening in the bushes and into the night. From a distance, she heard a crash, but she was too scared to stop and investigate. Alex led her into a black forest, where the snow was so deep it made running almost impossible. There was no moon or stars to light the way, so she followed Alex blindly. Two bright eyes suddenly blinked at her from behind a tree and Lizzie froze.

"Come on," Alex said, "it's just a cat. You can't stop now." He grabbed her hand and pulled her through a clearing in the trees which led to Forest Avenue.

Shaking, Lizzie bent over to catch her breath. "Ah, thanks, Alex."

"It's okay." Alex grinned. "I heard about *The Plan*. And when I saw you walking with the guys, I kind of knew that they were up to something."

"What do you think happened? The crash? Back there?" Lizzie asked.

Alex shook his head. "I don't know. Maybe the guys knocked over some lights or a display or something." He kicked a chunk of snow, sending it down the sidewalk. "Want me to walk you home?"

Joy Lynn Goddard

"Ah, no, that's okay." Lizzie didn't want to be seen with Alex. He was weird. He didn't seem to have any friends, at least not in Lizzie's class. Lizzie lived on the same street as Emily, and she couldn't take a chance of being seen with Alex. "I have to go back to the arena and get my bag. Then I'm practically home."

"Oh, my bag's there too."

"Well, er . . ."

Alex turned away. He picked up a broken tree branch and pitched it into the wind. He was always moving. It was strange. "I'll get my bag tomorrow," he said. "See ya," and he spun around and ran down Forest Avenue.

The street was deserted as she lugged her hockey bag past Emily's house and up the steps onto the verandah of her own house. Her mother was framed in the window, at the piano with Tony, a dark-haired nine-year-old who was one of her students. As Lizzie came through the door, Tony was playing "Ode to Joy" for what seemed like the hundredth time that month and still hitting a wrong note in the same bar each time.

He fidgeted on the piano bench.

"It's this note, Tony," Lizzie's mom said, hitting a piano key.

Tony clunked the song out again.

Lizzie was glad that her mother was too busy to look up to see the trouble written all over Lizzie's face. Her mother was good at spotting trouble, even when Lizzie hadn't said a word.

Hanging her coat in the front closet, Lizzie heard the key turning at the back door. Tom, the tenant, stomped into the back entrance, shaking snow from his boots.

"Hi Lizzie. What's up?"

"Not much. Cold out, eh?"

"Hmm . . ." Tom drew his eyebrows together and scratched his beard. "Something's going on at the Gallinas' house. The house with the big Christmas display?"

"Oh?"

"A couple of police cars are there, and there's a lot of commotion."

"Really?" Lizzie's heart was pounding so loudly she was scared it could be heard in the next room.

"It looks like vandalism. I didn't stay long to see. I've got a pile of work to do before tomorrow's class." Tom hung his coat on the peg by the back door and headed downstairs into his apartment.

After making a hot chocolate, Lizzie couldn't drink it. She jumped as the phone rang and the answering machine clicked on, with some carpet-cleaning business trying to sign up clients.

Lizzie's mother walked Tony to the front door and then joined Lizzie at the kitchen table.

"How was your day?" she asked.

"Good."

"And practice?"

"Fine." Avoiding her mother's eyes, Lizzie stirred the hot chocolate, working at a large lump of chocolate powder.

"Something wrong?"

"No, why?"

Her mother checked the clock on the kitchen wall. "You're late, and you look kind of strange."

"It's nothing, really."

The doorbell rang and Lizzie swallowed hard.

CHAPTER 4
YOU HAVE THE RIGHT TO REMAIN SILENT . . .

An icy wind blew into the kitchen as Lizzie's mother opened the door to a very large police officer in a blue uniform.

"Good evening, I'm Officer Gazzola from the City of Northview Police Department," he said, flashing his identification card. "I'm looking for Elizabeth Lockyer."

"Elizabeth?" With eyebrows raised, Laura turned briefly to the kitchen table where Lizzie sat in stunned silence. "This is Elizabeth, my daughter. I call her Lizzie. What, exactly, is this about?"

The officer frowned. "The Gallinas' property was vandalized a short time ago. Christmas lights were broken and the display was damaged. Apparently this set off a small fire. The fire department is over there right now. Two witnesses have identified your daughter as the person responsible."

"I didn't do anything!" Lizzie blurted, her heart racing as the colour drained out of her mother's face.

Officer Gazzola referred to his notes. "The two witnesses were Sean Trento and Trevor Watts."

"But, I can explain."

"You'll get your chance," he said briskly, as he stuck his notes into his pocket. "Both boys and their parents are on their way to the police station right now. You and your mother need to come along too. Get your coats and meet me in the patrol car."

The police station, a tall, gray building on the corner of Wyndham and Church streets, was windowless, except for a few slits rimming the top floor. It had seemed like such a friendly place when Lizzie had taken a class trip there in Grade Two – when the officers had been introduced as the good people who protected little children from the bad people – but now the station seemed like such a frightening place.

At the front counter, an officer was scowling over a pile of paperwork, and at a desk nearby, another officer was barking orders into the phone. Officer Gazzola directed Lizzie and her mother to a seat in the lobby and then disappeared behind a door. While a police officer led a handcuffed teenager to the back of the building, Lizzie slid across the long wooden bench to get as close as she could to her mother.

Officer Gazzola hurried back to the lobby and led Lizzie and her mother down a long hall and into a windowless room. Trevor and his mother, along with Sean and his father, were sitting at the only table in the room. The table filled most of the room. Directly above it, a long electrical cord with a single socket and light bulb hung from the ceiling. Lizzie's favourite police show sprang to mind because it had a similar interrogation room. Swallowing hard, she imagined that next an officer would be reading her the rights, just like on TV: *"You have the right to remain silent . . ."*

While she and her mother took their seats at the table, Trevor stole a look at Lizzie. Sean looked down, fixing his attention on the scratches on the metal table top. Identifying himself as Officer Stamoes, a

DAREDEVILS

second police officer marched into the room, and he, along with Officer Gazzola, began the interrogation.

Resting his elbows on the table, Officer Stamoes looked briefly at his papers and then studied the children. "The Gallina family is very upset. Parts of their late son's memorial have been destroyed. Lights were smashed. There was an electrical fire. Now, let's get the whole story."

Trevor's mother cleared her throat. "My son says he saw Elizabeth Lockyer on the Gallinas' property when he was walking home from hockey practice."

"Yes, that's right," Sean's father said, nodding. "My boy was walking home with Trevor. They both saw Elizabeth steal one of the lights."

"That's not true!" Lizzie fought back tears, a lump stuck in her throat.

"Trevor, tell the officers exactly what you told me," Trevor's mother urged, crossing her arms with conviction.

"Lizzie, um, tried to steal Rudolph's nose. Sean and I saw her. We jumped over the gate to stop her, and that's when it happened."

Joy Lynn Goddard

"What happened?" Officer Gazzola flipped through his notes and peered over the top of his glasses at Trevor. "Let's hear the details."

"She fell off the stand where Rudolph was. And when she fell she smashed some lights." Trevor fixed his eyes on Sean. "Right, Sean?"

"Guess so." Sean continued to study the table top, avoiding any eye contact with the others in the room.

"I guess that's how the fire started." Trevor looked directly at Officer Gazzola. "With the lights breaking and all."

"I think it's time we heard Lizzie's side of things," Lizzie's mother said.

"Lizzie?" Officer Stamoes sat back. "Your turn."

"I didn't fall, and I didn't break anything." Lizzie sniffed, as tears started to fall, and she reached for the box of Kleenex that Officer Stamoes held out to her. "I was going to take Rudolph's nose. I admit it. But it was Sean and Trevor's plan. They dared me to do it. And when I got up on the stand to take it, I couldn't do it. I told Trevor and Sean to steal the nose themselves if they wanted it so much. Then I climbed down the ladder and ran when I heard a car coming. I didn't fall. I heard something breaking. But that was after I'd long gone. Honestly."

"So who's telling the truth?" Officer Stamoes looked around the table.

"That's the whole truth," Lizzie said, dabbing her eyes with a balled-up tissue. "You can ask Alex. He was there too. Alex Fabiano."

"Was he with the boys?" Officer Stamoes searched her face.

"No," Lizzie said. "He was by himself. He followed us to the Gallinas' and just watched. Then, when we heard a car coming, he helped me get away. Phone and ask him. Please."

Lizzie's mother leaned over and whispered something into Officer Gazzola's ear, then led Lizzie from the room. When they returned fifteen minutes later, Alex and his father had joined the others in the room.

"I just took my daughter to the washroom. I wanted to see if she had any bruises or cuts – or anything that might show that she had fallen –

specifically into some Christmas lights," said Lizzie's mother, looking pointedly at the two officers. "There wasn't a scratch anywhere."

Trevor's mother abruptly turned and glared at her son but didn't say a word.

"That seems to be likely, according to what Alex had to say," Officer Gazzola said. "Alex?"

"It's like I said. I followed Trevor, Sean and Lizzie to the Gallinas'. I'd heard the guys talking at the rink about a plan. Trevor and Sean told Lizzie to steal the nose. She didn't want to do it. She chickened out at the last minute. I heard a car and helped her get away. We'd almost reached the forest when we heard a big crash." He paused, staring blankly at the mud-coloured walls, as if thinking. "I thought the guys had tripped over the display or lights or something."

Trevor's mother suddenly banged the table. "Trevor, you told me that you hurt your leg. Start explaining."

"It's like I said before. I hurt it at hockey practice." Trevor was the best liar in the whole world, Lizzie decided. He could look someone right in the eye and make someone believe his big fat lie was the truth. Ms. Borlino seemed to accept the crazy excuses he gave for not having his homework done, but it seemed much harder for him to pull one over on his mother.

"I want the truth," said his mother, her eyes cold and pointy, like icicles.

Trevor slid down in his seat as far as he could and mumbled, "I tripped, um, over the display or something and fell. I smashed the lights by accident. It wasn't on purpose."

"Hmm, I can see all the pieces of this puzzle are falling into place," Officer Stamoes said, leaning back in his chair with his hands tucked behind his head. "It doesn't appear to be vandalism since the damage was not deliberate." He sat up suddenly, his jaw tightening. "However, you children were trespassing on private property, and as a result, a lot of damage was done. The Gallinas shouldn't have to pay for it. Not a penny."

"We'll pay, certainly," Trevor's mother said.

Joy Lynn Goddard

"We'll help." Sean's father looked at his son. "Start saving your allowance."

"What about community service?" Lizzie's mother turned to Officer Gazzola. "I'd like Elizabeth to shovel the Gallinas' driveway or to do some other things for the Gallinas. It's only right."

Lizzie's heart sank. Facing the Gallina's was going to be hard, maybe one of the hardest things she'd ever do. They were a kind, old couple who kept to themselves most of the time, except at Christmas, when they brought freshly baked cookies and fruitcake to the Lockyers' house and stayed for tea.

"Good idea." Officer Gazzola nodded.

"And I'd like Alex to do the same," Alex's father piped up, smiling at Lizzie and her mother from across the table. "After all, he was aiding and abetting a criminal."

CHAPTER 5
DA DUM, DA DUM, DA DUM, DA DUM . . .

Emily pushed her glasses back on her nose and frowned at Lizzie. "Your shirt looks kind of funny." They were standing in front of the long mirror that stretched across the sinks in the girls' bathroom at school. "Why don't you tuck it in?"

"That makes me look fat." Lizzie sighed, tucking her shirt into her jeans and turning from side to side in the mirror. "See. At least that's what Tara says."

"Tara?"

"You know. Pete's daughter."

"Oh *her*." Emily made a face like she'd just taken a bite out of a rotten apple. "What does she know? I wouldn't waste one minute listening to her. First of all, she's way too skinny – a scrawny toothpick if you ask me – and secondly, she's just trying to be mean."

Lizzie nodded. "Pete's always trying to get her to eat more, but she won't. At dinner I've seen her take a tiny portion of mashed potatoes and move it around on

Joy Lynn Goddard

her plate. Somehow she thinks this tricks her dad into believing she's eating a lot, yet she hardly eats a bite."

"It's crazy," Emily said. "Parents are always bent out of shape about their kids' eating habits. Either kids eat too much or not enough. Or they don't eat the right foods. My goofy brother refuses to eat anything but peanut butter and jelly sandwiches." Turning to the mirror, she drew her dark hair back and fastened it at the nape of her neck with a hair clip. With her glasses on and hair pulled back, she looked like a bookworm; the other kids called her the librarian's clone. It didn't help that she was almost as tall and as bony as St. Mark's librarian.

By contrast, Lizzie appeared short and stocky as she stood beside Emily in the bathroom mirror. There wasn't one ounce of fat on her bones, only muscle. "Speaking of food," she said, "Mom's making a special treat tonight because we're going to trim the tree and Tara . . ."

Her words were cut off when the bathroom door flew open and in rushed Lisa, Mary, Nicole and Jennifer.

DAREDEVILS

"Good," Mary said, eying Emily and Lizzie. "Now we have some more guests."

"Guests?" Emily asked.

"For the wedding," Lisa said.

"Wedding? Who's getting married?" Emily peered at the girls over the top of her glasses.

"Bruno and Brunella." Nicole grinned, batting her eyes.

Lisa pulled a plastic lizard, about fifteen centimetres long, out of her pocket. "Meet Bruno," she said, sticking the bright green toy with the black hat and bow tie in Emily's face.

"And this is Brunella." Mary held up another toy lizard. It was wrapped in white lace, with a tissue draped over its head that was secured by a rubber band; its long, skinny tail was the only part of its body that wasn't dressed.

"They're going to get married and have tiny green babies and live happily ever after," Lisa gushed.

Emily shot Lizzie a look. Everyone knew that Family Life was Lisa's favourite subject in school. "Aren't you taking this Family Life thing a bit far?"

Joy Lynn Goddard

Ignoring her, Lisa began to sing "The Wedding March" off key, "*Da dum, da dum; da dum, da dum.*" Mary, Jennifer and Nicole joined in as they marched over to the string of bathroom stalls and arranged themselves in a line. After tying a string around Brunella's neck, Mary slowly dragged the toy across the bathroom tiles towards Bruno, positioned under the bathroom window with sunlight streaming across its back.

"You mean, you're going to have a wedding right here, in the bathroom, next to the stinky stalls?" Lizzie held her nose. "And between two lizards?" She stole a look at Emily who was rolling her eyes. Lizzie and Emily had had many long talks about the other girls in their class, agreeing that they were a bit much to take sometimes. Most of the girls were boy crazy and cared about little else, except clothes and hanging around the mall, whereas Lizzie liked sports and Emily was wrapped up in books.

With a shrug, Lisa continued to sing "The Wedding March."

Mary cleared her throat loudly and began the ceremony. "Dearly beloved," she said, her head bowed, her hands together and pointed upward prayerfully, like a priest's, "we are gathered here in the sight of God to . . ."

Suddenly, a small furry creature dashed from under a stall, climbed over Mary's feet and darted between the two toy lizards. The missing hamster. Adam's hamster. The whole school had been looking for it.

Lisa screamed and clung to the top of a stall door, tucking her feet up as far as she could. "A rat. It's a rat!"

Jennifer, Nicole and Mary started screaming too, as they hopped all over the place. "It's not a rat," Emily cried. "It's a hamster. Stop shrieking like a bunch of idiots and help me catch it."

Emily grabbed a waste container and ran after the hamster. Just as she captured it, the bathroom door swung open and in walked Mrs. Salibo, the oldest and meanest teacher in the school. She taught the older kids down the hall from Lizzie's classroom and Lizzie dreaded the day that she got Mrs. Salibo for a teacher.

"What's all the racket about in here?" She scowled. "The lunch bell's already rung and you're supposed to get back to class."

"We caught the missing hamster," Lisa said. "It's in the waste can."

While Mrs. Salibo peered into the bin, Mary snatched up the toy lizards and quickly hid them inside her pockets. Everybody knew that Mrs. Salibo didn't care for nonsense.

"Poor thing. Looks frightened to death with all that noise," Mrs. Salibo said, her voice much softer now. "I'll take it back to Ms. Borlino's room. It's Adam's, right?"

"Yes," the girls piped up together.

"You girls get back to class now. You're going to be late."

The girls left the washroom and followed the steady stream of children hurrying in the halls towards classrooms.

At the water fountain, Trevor and Sean waited at the back of the line to take one last drink before the afternoon classes began. When they spotted Alex trudging down the wet, slushy hall with his head down, Trevor stuck out a boot and tripped him.

Stumbling, Alex fell into Trevor.

"Hey, watch where you're going," Sean cried, grabbing Alex's jacket and shoving him against the wall. "Somebody could get hurt, ya know." Then he shot Trevor a look.

Alex's face turned almost as red as his cherry-red hat and scarf. He shook himself free and hurried down the hall, saying nothing and looking at nobody.

Lizzie and Emily followed him through the classroom door. He shrugged off his coat, then took his seat in stony silence. Something deep down in the pit of Lizzie's stomach started to simmer, like a pot of water on the stove that gets hotter and hotter until it bubbles into hissing steam. She tramped over to Alex's desk. "Don't let those guys push you around."

Alex looked up, brushing hair from his eyes. "Huh?"

"Trevor. Sean. They're big idiots."

Alex shrugged. "No problem. I'm okay."

Lizzie let out a deep breath, the steam evaporating. Shoving her hands in her pockets, she eyeballed the black scuffs across the toes of her white running shoes. "Ah, thanks again for helping me."

"Hmm?" Alex picked up a pencil and started doodling on his notebook.

"The other day? For telling the police that I didn't break the lights."

"Sure." His brown eyes were warm, like chocolate.

"We found Adam's hamster," Lizzie said, knowing that Alex would be happy to hear the news since he'd been looking for the hamster for ages. "It was in the washroom. Mrs. Salibo came in and . . ."

Silence had blanketed the classroom. The usual noise after lunch of kids taking off boots and coats, finding books and getting ready for the next lesson had disappeared. When Lizzie looked around, all eyes were fixed on her with Alex, the weird kid.

"Well, gotta go." She dashed to her desk and slid down, hiding behind her hair.

DAREDEVILS

Pushing up from her desk, Ms. Borlino told the kids to take out their math books and turn to the chapter on fractions.

Willy groaned.

"What's the problem?" Ms. Borlino asked, an eyebrow raised. "Fractions aren't so bad."

"They're hard," Willy said.

"Well, just lōok at them this way," Ms. Borlino said, turning to the board. With chalk she drew a large circle on the board with strokes crisscrossing through it, like spokes in a wheel. Pointing to the drawing, she swung back to the class. "This is a pizza. I've divided it into ten pieces." She shaded one piece of the pizza with chalk. "I've decided to give one piece to Alex. What part of the pizza have I given away? Alex?"

"Pardon me?" Alex stared at the board.

"What part of the pizza have I shaded in?"

Quickly searching for an answer, Alex flipped through his text.

Ms. Borlino took a deep breath and let it out very slowly. "The answer's on the board, not in the book. Alex, please pay attention."

Alex was constantly in trouble for not paying attention. Lizzie couldn't count the many times she'd heard teachers tell Alex that he was in spaceland; Ms. Borlino was the exception. She was really nice, but even she got mad at Alex the time the class went to the conservation area to study nature and Alex got lost because he wasn't listening to the instructions. The whole class spent hours looking for him. Ms. Borlino was about to call the police when she found him right smack in the middle of a rushing stream, in a restricted area, catching water bugs in a net. When Ms Borlino yelled at him, he wore a blank look on his face, as if he couldn't understand what the fuss was all about.

Hoping the class would stop gawking at Alex, Lizzie shot up her hand, ready with the answer for Ms. Borlino's math question on fractions. "One-tenth. There's one-tenth of the pizza shaded in."

"Good."

Fractions were easy and kind of boring, thought Lizzie, her mind drifting to other things; she spent a lot of time daydreaming in school because she found most subjects boring. Most of the day she wished that school were over and that she could move on to more interesting things, like hockey. This day, though, was different. After school, she was going to shovel snow at the Gallinas', and she wasn't looking forward to that.

When the bell rang, she didn't rush out the door with all the other kids. She took plenty of time eating her peanut butter and banana sandwich leftover from lunch, and then she shoved her lunch kit, math textbook and pencil case into her bookbag for home. Reaching for her coat, she felt a tap on her shoulder. Alex. His coat hook was at the other end. Lizzie assumed he was going to ask her about homework; he probably hadn't listened to the teacher. Instead, he asked, "Are you going to the Gallinas' after school?"

Lizzie nodded, pulling on a boot. "How'd you know?"

"My dad phoned your mom. Want to go together?"

She quickly looked around the class. She didn't want anyone to think she had a thing for Alex, the weird kid. Nobody was watching, except Emily, who usually walked home with her.

"The Gallinas'?" Emily raised an eyebrow. "Why are you going there?"

"Remember? I have to shovel snow because I got in trouble with the police and all."

"Oh, right," Emily shrugged. "See you later."

"Bye." Lizzie flung her bookbag over her shoulder and turned to Alex. "Let's go."

Clumping across the snow-covered football field, they hardly spoke. Lizzie thought hard for something to say. It was hard making conversation with a boy. With Emily, she talked nonstop about school and teachers and the girls in the class that were particularly annoying, for it was easy to talk to Emily.

Turning into the catwalk, a shortcut to Greenway Drive and the Gallinas' property, Lizzie swallowed hard. "Ms. Borlino's pretty cool. Don't you think?"

"Guess so, as far as teachers go." Alex glanced at the barking dogs, fenced in on the property that skirted the catwalk.

Lizzie cleared her throat to get his attention and thought of a new topic, hockey. She loved discussing the national hockey teams with Pete, her mother's boyfriend. "Think the Leafs will make the playoffs?"

"Dunno."

"What's your favourite team?"

Alex didn't answer, and Lizzie wondered if he'd heard her. Despite the biting wind whipping snow in her face, Lizzie was hot and clammy.

Suddenly Alex swung his bookbag off his shoulder and hunkered down to unzip it. On the snow-covered walkway he dumped a pencil case, a binder and a lunch container, all with the Montreal Canadiens crest on them. "The Canadiens," he grinned, his eyes bright. "They're the best."

Alex stared at Lizzie. "How come you play on a boys' team?"

Lizzie had heard this question a lot. "Cause there's no good girls' team in Northview. I mean, there are some House League teams, but there's no Rep team, like the Tigers. Northview's too small, I guess." She shrugged.

Joy Lynn Goddard

"Oh."

They slowly walked up the Gallinas' driveway and lifted the brass knocker that was in the centre of the door. Lizzie had already apologized to the Gallinas for the damage to their Christmas display, but she still felt a little embarrassed seeing them face to face again.

When Mrs. Gallina opened the door, a blast of warm air escaped with the aroma of baked bread. "Right on time." Her eyes twinkled. "You'll find two shovels in the shed in the back. And when you're finished, please stop in for a hot chocolate."

"Thanks, Mrs. Gallina," Lizzie said. "But I have to get home right after I've finished. We're trimming the tree."

While Alex started shoveling from the bottom of the driveway, Lizzie took the part nearest the back door. After working for well over an hour, the children met in the middle to finish the job. Working together made the job much easier, thought Lizzie, watching Alex fling his last shovel of snow over the bank and then flop backward on the snowy front yard.

"Come on, Lizzie. Let's make snow angels," he cried.

Laughing, she fell backward into a pillow of snow next to Alex and waved her arms and legs. "Mine's better than yours."

Alex jumped up and pitched a snowball at her, hitting her smack on the head. "Snowball fight!"

Scrambling to her feet, Lizzie pelted him with one snowball after the other until he cried for mercy. It was so much fun that she asked Alex to come home with her to trim the tree.

CHAPTER 6
OF TALL TALES AND TARA

The house was warm and smelled of cinnamon and hot apple cider as Lizzie and Alex walked inside and kicked off their boots. After laying their wet hats and gloves on the floor register to dry, they wandered into the living room. Alex headed straight to the fire crackling in the hearth and warmed his hands, while Lizzie called out to her mother. There was no answer. "The First Noel" was playing softly from the CD player in the entertainment centre next to the couch. A very large tree, bare yet of trimmings, filled the room with a pine scent.

Alex stared at the tree, his head back. "That's a big one!"

"My mom likes to get the biggest tree she can find, and they're always real too," Lizzie said. She remembered the Christmases when she and her mother had lived in the apartment across the city and weren't allowed to have real trees because the landlord said that they were a fire hazard. Year after year, her mother would put up a spindly artificial tree that had been kept in a box in the storage room for most of the year, folded up like a pretzel. Each year it was missing more green plastic strands on its wire branches. Her mother always smiled and pretended that the tree didn't matter, but Lizzie could tell that it did, because her mother sighed softly every time she put it in the stand. "We had a hard time dragging it in the house, but Pete helped. He's mom's boyfriend," she said.

Lizzie led Alex into the kitchen and scooped some hot apple cider from the crock-pot and poured it into large mugs. While climbing on stools at the counter, they heard soft laughter coming from another room and swung around. Inside the archway to the dining room, Laura and Pete were kissing under the mistletoe.

Lizzie didn't dare look at Alex, certain her face was as bright red as Rudolph's nose. She cleared her throat. "I'm home."

"I'm afraid you caught us at a weak moment," Pete said, breaking away from Laura, his eyes flitting to the ball of green leaves with white, waxy berries that was hanging in the archway. "The mistletoe and all." He grinned.

Laura took a step into the kitchen. "Alex, isn't it? Welcome to our home. Pete, this is the boy who was such a big help to Lizzie at the police station. Remember? I told you all about that mess."

Pete nodded. "Good to meet you," he said, shaking Alex's hand. "And thanks for helping *our* Lizzie." Pete's *our* made Lizzie feel special, like the time she was home sick with pneumonia and a whole pile of get-well cards arrived from the kids in her class.

"How was the shoveling?" Laura lifted the lid on the crock-pot and stirred the cider, filling the room with the aroma of cinnamon.

"It took us about an hour," Lizzie said. "And Mrs. Gallina invited us in for hot chocolate, but we said no because of trimming the tree and all."

"Well, I'm glad you invited Alex along to help," Laura said in her ordinary, everyday voice, as if Lizzie brought a boy home many times a week. "We're going to get started as soon as Tara, Pete's daughter, arrives."

Pete checked his watch, frowning. "It looks like she's almost an hour late."

"She probably met up with one of her friends," Laura said. "Don't worry, she'll be here soon."

Laura headed into the living room carrying two large bowls, one filled with fresh popcorn, the other with cranberries, and she set them on the coffee table. To each child she handed a large darning needle threaded with string, and everyone began stringing popcorn and cranberries to decorate the tree.

Pete was peeking through the window blinds into the dark street when his daughter arrived at the Lockyers' door with a tall, pimply boy.

"This is Phil," she said, barely glancing at the boy. "He's from school."

Phil moved his lips but said nothing. He shoved his hands into his grungy coat and stared at his thick, gray socks, one with a hole in the toe.

After introductions were made all around, Pete glared at his daughter. "Where were you? You're over an hour late."

"Well, we got talking and we lost track of time."

Lizzie couldn't imagine Phil talking at all – he still hadn't said a word.

Pete looked from Laura to his daughter. "Do you think maybe an apology is in order?"

Tara let out a heavy sigh. "Oh, sorry and all that."

"That's fine," Laura said. "Apology accepted. We just got started with the decorations. We're stringing popcorn and cranberries. Perhaps Phil would like to help us?"

"Oh, we're going to the mall. We can't stay," Tara said, and she started to zip up her ski jacket.

"The mall?" Pete tensed, the cords on his neck suddenly popping out. "Tara, the plan was that you were to come here and give us a hand with the tree. We made these arrangements yesterday. Now you're changing your plans and without asking me first."

Laura rested a hand on Pete's shoulder. "That's okay if she wants to go to the mall."

Pete shook his head, avoiding Laura's eyes. "She needs to be more considerate. She's got to learn to follow through with plans – not change in mid-direction without consulting me first."

"Yes, well, I guess you're probably right." Laura blushed.

The room fell silent. Laura pressed a button on the CD player and "I Saw Mommy Kissing Santa Claus" filled the room.

"What about a compromise here?" Pete asked his daughter. "You and Phil stay for a while and help with the tree, and then I'll drive you to the mall."

Tara shrugged. "I guess."

Pete seemed happy until Tara took off her hat. "What the . . . ?"

A strip of Tara's long dark brown hair – running from her crown down the back of her head – was bleached yellow, like straw.

Lizzie and Alex, exchanging looks, burst out laughing.

"She looks like a skunk," Lizzie laughed. "Just like a . . ."

Joy Lynn Goddard

One look from Laura and Lizzie froze.

Pete's mouth was open but he said nothing, his face a sickly, chalk-white, as if he'd just eaten something that didn't agree with him. He took Tara into another room while Laura tried to interest the others in stringing cranberries and popcorn.

The voices drifting from the other room were followed by long silences. There was no yelling, and Lizzie was relieved because yelling always gave her a huge stomachache. Everybody yelled at Emily's house. Once she was there for dinner and there was so much yelling that she couldn't eat a bite, and the fuss was about nothing: someone drank the last of the milk and put the empty container in the fridge.

A long time passed before Tara hunkered back to the living room hiding behind her skunk hair. Phil glanced up briefly as she sat down on the couch beside him and then went back to stringing cranberries and popcorn. The pattern on each string was supposed to be two cranberries, followed by one piece of popcorn. Everyone in the room was following the pattern, except Phil. He was stringing one cranberry, two pieces of popcorn. Laura pointed out that Phil was showing an artistic difference and then took his string and draped it at the top of the tree.

Alex couldn't sit still long enough to complete his string of cranberries and popcorn. He seemed more interested in climbing the ladder and decorating the top half of the tree with green and red glass balls.

Laura left the room and came back carrying a small angel. Lizzie had made the ornament for her mother in Grade Two, dutifully keeping it a secret until Christmas morning. The angel's white lace was tattered and its styrofoam head a bit askew now, years later, but Laura always stared at it with the same dreamy look she'd had on the Christmas Day she unwrapped it, saying it was the most beautiful angel in the whole world. Insisting that it shouldn't be hidden in a box until Christmas each year, Laura kept it on a shelf in the dining room year round.

"Time to put the angel on top of the tree," Laura said. "Are you ready Lizzie?"

Lizzie held the angel. She wanted to believe that there were real angels, like the kind pictured on the stained-glass windows at church – but she wasn't certain. She had learned about angels at school, especially guardian angels, and she felt some comfort believing that there might be someone or something looking out for her. "Here, you put it on top," she said, handing the angel to Alex on the ladder. "You're closer."

Alex stood up carefully. Hooking his foot underneath a rung, he reached to the top of the tree with the angel and just barely slipped it on when the ladder started to slide. Pete jumped up from the couch and steadied the ladder, holding on to Alex, but the tree toppled over. Glass shards from the red and green balls scattered across the carpet.

Laura and Pete quickly determined that no one was hurt and then burst out laughing. With an arm around Laura, Pete sang a few bars of "O Christmas Tree" in a deep, warm voice. "Not exactly an ideal tree-trimming party." He grinned.

Tara rolled her eyes. "The pits."

"Not everything's broken," Lizzie said, bouncing up with the angel, its head on the same crooked angle as before, its halo intact.

"And no one was hurt." Laura smiled at Alex, looking him over once more for signs of injury. "Not a scratch. You must have a guardian angel."

With a shrug, he hunkered down to clean up the broken Christmas decorations at his feet, while Lizzie couldn't help wondering if Alex really did have a guardian angel. Coming to mind was the time at the conservation area when he'd been lost for many hours and found unharmed, and the many times on the ice when he had been hit by a puck or had been slammed hard into the boards, and he always managed to have nothing more than a couple of bruises to show for the rough games.

Lizzie helped him clean up the mess, and then Alex headed for home. Soon after, as promised, Pete took Tara and Phil to the mall while Lizzie and her mother finished trimming the tree.

Joy Lynn Goddard

The soft tap on the bedroom door startled Lizzie. It was dark in the room, except for the thin stream of light from the night stand, as Lizzie curled up in bed with a book. She had just come to the scary part in the story – where ghosts were swooping throughout the haunted castle – when there was a knock at the door.

"Come in."

Her mother stood in the doorway at a loss for words.

Thoughts of the ghosts vanished, but Lizzie's heart continued to race as she studied the weird look on her mother's face.

"What's wrong?"

"Hmm, nothing," her mother said. "I just want you to come downstairs for a few minutes and talk."

Lizzie scrambled off the bed and followed her mother down the stairs silently, wondering why Laura seemed so strange all of a sudden. She had been fine earlier, trimming the tree. In fact she'd been in a really good mood. She loved Christmas.

Laura started playing with her gold earring as soon as she walked into the living room and sat down on the couch, a sure sign that something was wrong. She always played with her earrings when she was nervous, like the time she showed up at Lizzie's school early to break the news that Lizzie's grandmother had died.

Pete stood in front of the fire in the hearth, an arm stretched across the mantle. Tara was gone. Lizzie assumed that she was still at the mall or had gone home. Lizzie sat down on the couch next to her mother and hugged a throw cushion to her chest.

Searching her mother's face, then Pete's, she waited for someone to speak.

"We have something really important to tell you, Lizzie," her mother said, finally, as she turned and smiled softly at Pete.

Pete pulled the rocking chair next to the couch and sat down. "And we're hoping you will be happy with what we're going to say," he said.

"As you know, Pete and I have been seeing each other for a very long time," said Laura. "Well, we've fallen in love."

Joy Lynn Goddard

"And we want to get married." Pete's blue eyes were warm and they crinkled at the corners as he smiled at Lizzie.

Laura searched Lizzie's face. "We want to live here, together, as a family. What do you think?"

"Well . . ." Lizzie lowered her eyes to the carpet, to a glass shard missed earlier during clean up that was now glimmering by the fire. She was all mixed up. She liked Pete, but she wasn't sure that she wanted to share her mother with him or anyone else. She'd never had to share her mother with anyone. She looked briefly at Pete. "What should I call you?"

He squeezed her hand. "Just Pete, if that makes you comfortable."

"When, um, are you getting married?"

"Not 'til April," Lizzie's mother said. "We have a few preparations to make."

"Is it going to be a big wedding in the church with flowers and music and everything?" The idea didn't sound so bad after all, and Lizzie's excitement grew.

"Yes and no," said her mother. "We're planning a wedding with flowers and food and everything. But it will be small. Modest. After all, this is a second wedding for both of us. Ah, there is one more thing." Her hand reached for the gold earring again.

Pete took a deep breath and let it out slowly. "Tara may be coming to live with us. As you know, she lives with her mother. But her mother is planning to move away with her new husband, and Tara doesn't want to leave her friends and school and everyone else behind."

Lizzie felt like someone had punched her in the stomach. Tara. Skunk hair. Blue nails. Creepy friends. Loud music. Nothing but trouble. "Oh."

"Of course, there's going to be an adjustment," said Lizzie's mother. "But we'll all adjust together. You'll see."

Lizzie had had all the news she could stand. "Can I go back upstairs now?"

"Of course," her mother replied, her eyes wary. "You give this some thought. We'll talk later when you've had a chance to take it all in." Then she leaned over and kissed Lizzie's cheek.

With the throw cushion still clutched to her chest, even tighter now, Lizzie jumped up from the couch and ran up the stairs as if chased by a herd of wild animals.

CHAPTER 7
HE SHOOTS, HE SCORES

The wooden stands surrounding the rink in Northview Community Centre were packed with fans in crazy hats and bright, bulky coats, some with megaphones or banners, and others with faces painted their favourite team colours, all excited to see the Northview Tigers play the North Lake Hawks. Both teams were good. They'd played each other five times in the season so far, with the Tigers winning three games and losing two. If the Tigers won this game, they'd be competing in the finals in Niagara Falls and the Hawks would be out for the season. Lizzie could hardly breathe from the pressure building in her chest.

In the stands, just under the scoreboard, her mother was sitting with Pete and Tara. Long gone was Tara's skunk hair, for Pete had made her dye it back to its original colour, dark brown. Her hair fell in smooth curls across her shoulders, and it was kept in place by a small, fuzzy orange hat. She looked funky, not weird, and Lizzie heaved a sigh of relief. Everyone at school knew by now that Lizzie's mother was getting married to Tara's father and that Tara was going to become Lizzie's stepsister. She was now invited to come along on family outings, even though she seemed about as thrilled by the invitations as a kid who has to go to the dentist.

Nicole, Jennifer, Mary and Lisa were fooling around in the stands as Lizzie headed to the dressing room. They didn't even like hockey; they came to the games because they were just plain boy crazy. They cheered and giggled and acted crazy over Sean, Willy, Trevor and some of the other Tigers, but they didn't seem to know much about the game, and they thought Lizzie was really weird for wanting to play.

She set her bag on a bench in the dressing room, with plans to suit up after the coach's pep talk, and then she hurried to the coaches' circle in the anteroom.

Willy and Ricky and some of the other players were already there, laughing, joking and fooling around. As usual, Lizzie felt left out. The Tigers ignored her most of the time, all except Alex. Although she was their goalie, the players rarely included her in any of the fun or celebrations after a win and only paid attention to her when the team lost. Lizzie took a seat on the bench near Alex, sliding over for Trevor and Sean, who came in late.

Standing in the circle, Coach Powers brought the team to attention. Hands on his hips, he studied each face and was all business. "If we expect to beat the Hawks, we must play as a team and work together to win. There's no room for hotshots. Remember, Mario Lemieux is a team player and that's one of the reasons he's such a superstar in the NHL. He runs his team that way too."

Lizzie stole a look at Trevor. Mario Lemieux was his hero. He talked about him all the time, more than any other player, calling him "Super Mario" like the rest of the world. He watched videos and read a pile of books about him and just couldn't get enough of him. Just like his dad, Trevor thought Lemieux was the best player ever, and Trevor wanted to be just like him one day. Still, Trevor was not a team player like his hero. He was nothing but a big puck hog.

Joy Lynn Goddard

The Coach drew some diagrams on the chalkboard and talked for another ten minutes before dismissing the Tigers to dress for the game. Lizzie unzipped her bag and started to empty it. Chest pads, blocker and catching glove, extra socks. No mask. She checked again. Still, no mask. Coach Powers would never in a million years let her to play without a mask because it was against regulations. She swallowed hard.

She checked her watch. The game was starting in a few minutes. She dug around in the bottom of her bag again, hoping against reason that she'd find the mask there. She had to play. This wasn't fair. She knew she had packed the mask. She always checked and double checked that she had all her stuff before she left for a game; her mother made sure of it. Fighting back tears, she went back to the anteroom to tell the coach that she couldn't find the mask. The other players were there, sitting on the benches, dressed and ready.

"Lizzie? You're not dressed?" The coach raised an eyebrow. "What's up?"

"I, um . . ." Her throat was dry.

"Forget something?" Sean asked as he eyeballed Trevor. "You look kinda pale."

"Oh, my gosh," Trevor said, his eyes wide and his hands on his cheeks. "She forgot her makeup. She can't go without her makeup. What's the other team gonna think?"

"That's enough boys." Coach Powers glared. "Keep the sarcasm to yourselves."

"I can't find my mask," Lizzie said. "And I know I packed it."

"Are you sure?" The coach shook his head. "You know the rules, Lizzie. I can't let you play without proper protection. You could lose a tooth or worse." His eyes softened with sympathy.

She sniffed, determined not to cry, especially in front of the others. She wouldn't give them the satisfaction.

Using his best-behaviour voice, the one he reserved for teachers and coaches, Trevor asked, "Do you want me in net, coach? I'm backup."

Coach Powers glanced at the clock on the wall and let out a heavy sigh. "No time to . . . guess so, Trevor.

Sorry Lizzie." He gently placed a hand on her shoulder. "To show your team support, suit up but stay on the bench."

The Tigers slid onto the ice to warm up. Alone, in the players' box, Lizzie felt like the whole world was gawking at her, wondering why she wasn't playing with the team. Would the fans think she wasn't good enough to play in this key game? She tried to hide by scrunching down on the bench and letting her hair flow like a curtain around her face, but she still stuck out for all to see.

This was the second time that she couldn't play this season. She'd had pneumonia the first time. Despite her mother's fussing, with chicken soup and ice cream brought to Lizzie's room on a fancy silver tray, and the pile of cards arriving at the door from the kids at school, it had been torture staying in bed and missing the game.

If she missed a third game, she'd be out of the finals. Her stomach tied up in knots. The coach benched any player who missed three games – that was the limit – and he made no exceptions. Another missed game and her dream would never come true. She tried hard to forget it, especially now, but the dream sprang to mind anyway:

To celebrate the end of the season, the Tigers have gathered in the banquet hall with the other teams from the Niagara Falls tournament. The players, with their families and friends, are sitting at large round tables that are draped with white linen tablecloths. On each table, is a vase with a single red carnation. Everybody is eating roast beef and mashed potatoes with rich, brown gravy and toasting each other with root beer – Lizzie's favourite soda pop.

As the dream continues, the coaches, one by one, walk up to the podium and tell everyone how well each team has played. Coach Powers talks about what fine players he has and how proud he is that the Tigers have won the tournament. He smiles, and after a long, nail-biting pause, announces the tournament's Most Valuable Goalie – and it's Lizzie Lockyer. The applause is deafening. With all eyes on her, Lizzie walks to the podium to accept her trophy. Her teammates suddenly stand up and make such a big fuss over her; they're so glad that she's part of the team....

She clears a spot for the trophy in her room. She puts it on the white shelf just above her desk where the glow from the light nearby will shine on its silver-plated goalie, which is fastened on top of its wooden stand. The trophy sits next to the small plaque that she won on Track and Field Day and close to the framed newspaper pictures of her hockey team.

The dream disappeared as thundering applause in the arena brought Lizzie back to reality. Trevor, in net, had just caught the puck.

Shouting their approval, fans held hands and jumped up and down in their seats, creating a wave across the stands.

Trevor strutted in the crease, like a peacock spreading its bright tail feathers in hopes of attracting a peahen. Although she couldn't see his face behind his mask, Lizzie was certain, knowing Trevor, that he wore an annoying, self-satisfied grin. And knowing Trevor, he probably believed that he was the best goalie in the whole world, better than Lizzie. He was bigger – the biggest kid in the class – and he was good at blocking the puck from the sides, but Lizzie was faster, and she kept more pucks out of the net. Still, like a dog with a bone, she couldn't let go of the fear that Trevor might steal her place in the net.

She couldn't hold back the tears any longer and they spilled down her cheeks, hot against her skin, despite the cold air in the rink. Sniffing, she wiped her face with her sleeve; she'd just die if anyone saw her bawling like a little kid. All eyes, however, were turned towards the Hawks' net, where Alex had just scored a goal. With the score tied 1-1, the third period was about to begin.

Deciding that she'd shown enough support for the Tigers, Lizzie left the players' box and clunked in her

Joy Lynn Goddard

skates across the floorboards to the dressing room. After changing, she headed down a set of stairs to the concession stand for a cup of hot chocolate.

Pushing through a set of glass doors, something in the corner of the stairwell caught her eye. It was small and white – a mask. Its chin guard was hanging askew, as if the mask had been thrown on the ground.

Lizzie rushed to pick it up. Inside on the label in black ink, in her mother's scratchy handwriting, was the name Lizzie Lockyer.

Her mind raced. Had she dropped the mask in the stairwell? No, impossible. She'd shoved it in the bag with the rest of her equipment and had been careful to zip up the bag. Someone had purposely dumped the mask there. She quickly looked around for answers. There was no one was in sight, except Mr. Murphy, at the concession booth just beyond the glass doors. She ran up to him and held up the mask. "Did you see anyone throw this under the stairwell?"

Mr. Murphy handed a hot dog to a customer and turned to Lizzie. "What's that?"

DAREDEVILS

"My mask. Somebody dumped it under the stairs. Did you see anyone suspicious?"

He scratched the few remaining hairs on his head and grunted, "Kids. Parents pay good money for things and kids just don't appreciate them. Kids have everything these days. Why, when I was a kid I had absolutely . . ."

Lizzie interrupted, "But did you see anyone?"

He shook his head. "No. Been busy right up 'til game time. I didn't see a thing."

As the buzzer sounded the end of the game, Lizzie hurried back to the rink. At the far end of the ice, over the net, the scoreboard flashed the results: a tie game, 1-1. This meant that the Tigers would be playing the Hawks again. She leaned her hands against the Plexiglass surrounding the rink and watched as the Tigers formed a line and shook hands with each player in the Hawks' line.

The anteroom was filled with noise and activity as she walked in carrying her mask; Coach Powers was excitedly discussing the game with parents, and the boys were congratulating each other with slaps on the back and dousing their sweat-soaked heads with bottles of water.

As she headed to the coach to show him the mask, Lizzie caught pointy looks from Trevor and Sean who were huddled together on a bench.

"Thought I hid it," Trevor mumbled.

"Right, under the stairs. You told me."

She stopped cold in her tracks and glared at the boys. "What did you say?"

Trevor smirked. "I was just saying to Sean that you found your mask. Too bad you didn't have it for the game. Did you drop it somewhere?"

Lizzie could hardly speak. Later, much later, she could probably find the right words to tell the boys exactly what she thought of them, but in the heat of the moment the words stuck in her throat like dry toast.

"Are you deaf or something?" Trevor kicked her boot. "I said . . ."

Lizzie found her voice. "I know what you said. And no, I didn't drop my mask somewhere. You dumped it under the stairwell. Didn't you?"

DAREDEVILS

"Prove it," Trevor said, with a laugh that made the hairs on the back of Lizzie's neck stand on end.

She couldn't prove it, and even if she could, she couldn't tell the coach. Players didn't tattle because if they did, they'd get nothing but the cold shoulder from the other players. And Lizzie had had enough of the cold shoulder.

Alex waved Lizzie over to his bench.

"Trevor did it," she said, plopping beside him and dumping her mask in her lap. "He threw my mask under the stairs. I heard him telling Sean."

"Shh, quiet." Alex leaned closer to Lizzie and whispered in her ear, "I think I've got a plan to get him back." Pulling her from the bench, he led the way to the door. "Tell you all about it when we're sure there are no big ears around."

CHAPTER 8
TIT FOR TAT

Tara was on the phone, sprawled across the couch in the family room with her smelly sneakers planted on the upholstery. If Lizzie had put her shoes on the furniture, her mother would have thrown a fit – but Tara got away with it. Her mother was constantly telling Lizzie, "Let's help Tara feel welcome here. We can't sweat the small stuff."

Tara wasn't even living with the Lockyers yet, but she'd already taken over the house. She was over often, at least three or four times a week, even without her dad, because Lizzie's mother and Tara's dad thought the visits would help with blending their families after the wedding. Although Lizzie wished with all her heart that Tara would move away with her own mother and stepfather, this wasn't going to happen; Tara had refused to leave her friends and school and Northview. Laura said that Lizzie would just have to learn to adjust to her stepsister.

Tara had been hogging the phone for an hour and getting louder and louder by the minute, when Lizzie, who was sitting on the floor, slid closer to the television and turned up the volume.

"Hey, Lizard, turn down the TV. I can't hear Phil," Tara cried.

"My name is Lizzie, not Lizard," Lizzie muttered under her breath, because complaining out loud about the nickname seemed to encourage Tara to use it all the more. Gritting her teeth, Lizzie turned off the set – she couldn't hear it anyway – and then, finishing her snack, she went to her room for some peace and quiet.

Tara wasn't allowed to put one toe in Lizzie's room, and Laura had made that quite clear. After the wedding, Tara was moving into the small bedroom that overlooked the backyard, which was next to the bathroom and at the far end of the hall from Lizzie's room. Laura had been hanging yellow-flowered wallpaper in the room and painting the furniture white, transforming the room from drab to sunny and fresh. Tara's father had moved a new bed in the room and was busy making a desk. Lizzie couldn't imagine Tara working at a desk. She'd probably just pile all her junk on it.

Lizzie had an old wooden desk that her mother had bought from a secondhand shop downtown. It was much too big for the small room and had a lot of scratches on it, but Lizzie loved it, especially its secret drawer, a small, thin compartment that was tucked underneath the main drawer and could only be opened with a skeleton key. She locked her most private possessions there, like her autobiography (a school project) and notes to Emily, and then she hid the key under a plant pot on top of the desk for safekeeping.

Tara left after dinner, and Lizzie let out a big sigh of relief – now Tara couldn't stick her nose in Lizzie's business. Alex was on his way to the house to talk about his plan to get even with Trevor. He had come up with some ideas earlier, and now he was ready with the rest.

As he joined her on the couch in the family room, Lizzie was all ears.

"Trevor thinks he's the best hockey player in the whole world, right?" Alex raised an eyebrow. "Well, we're gonna show him just how great he is."

"How are we going to do that?"

A hint of a smile crossed Alex's face. "Let's pretend that there was a hockey scout at the Tigers' last game, and that this scout is a cousin of Trevor's hero, Mario Lemieux."

"Okay." Lizzie nodded.

"And let's say, that this scout tells Super Mario all about Trevor – that Trevor's the best player he's seen in a long, long time."

"Trevor's the only one who thinks he's great," Lizzie said, rolling her eyes. "He's so full of himself."

Grinning, Alex jumped up and started pacing in front of the couch. "Let's say that Lemieux's planning to sponsor a young hockey player, like Trevor. He wants to give him a bunch of tips 'til he's ready for the NHL. Everybody knows that Lemieux's always doing nice things for people, like charity work and stuff."

"So, I get it," Lizzie said, sitting back on the couch and drawing a foot under her leg. "We're going to tell

Trevor that Mario Lemieux, Super Mario, top scorer, the guy who has won two Stanley Cups and has been inducted in the Hall of Fame, Mr. Hockey himself, wants to sponsor him?" She groaned, tossing her head back. "Trevor will never believe it in a million years."

"Hmm . . ." Alex stared into space. "He'll believe it – if we send him an official-looking letter from Lemieux's cousin, the scout."

"Okay, then what?" Lizzie waited.

"Well, the letter will tell Trevor to meet the scout at the arena to discuss the details, and that Trevor's not to tell his friends about the meeting because they'll want to get in on the action too."

"Knowing Trevor, he'll do the opposite and blab to the whole world," Lizzie cried.

"I'm counting on it." Alex sank back on the couch and smirked. "And then everybody will show up at the rink, hoping to see Trevor with Lemieux's cousin, the scout."

"And there won't be a scout."

"And Trevor will look like a jerk," Alex said, his eyes wide.

"A big jerk," Lizzie laughed, clapping a "high five" with her friend.

Then they sat down at the computer to write the letter. While Lizzie typed, Alex pretended to be the scout, Andrew Long, a name he'd dreamed up using the first initial in both his and Lizzie's names:

Dear Trevor:

Coach Powers gave me your name. I am a hockey scout who has seen you play a couple of times. You are a great player, strong and aggressive, like a Tiger should be. You have the potential to go places. I've told my cousin, Mario Lemieux, about your skills and he'd like to sponsor you. This will help you get in the NHL when you're older. If you are interested, I will meet you at the arena to discuss the details at 4:30 p.m., Tuesday, Jan. 31. Please don't tell your friends about this meeting because they might want Mr. Lemieux to

Joy Lynn Goddard

> *sponsor them too. He's only prepared to sponsor one player. Thank you.*
> *Sincerely,*
> *Andrew Long*

It was Tuesday, the day Trevor was supposed to meet the "scout." Lizzie and Alex had slipped the letter into Trevor's mail slot that morning, first waiting for his parents to go to work so they wouldn't mess up the plan. Leaning on the desk, with her chin in her hand, Lizzie stared at Ms. Borlino at the front of the room, half listening to her lesson on nutrition. It was hard to concentrate on schoolwork when all she could think about was Alex's plan. Did Trevor get the letter? Did he believe it? Did he tell the other kids? A hundred things could go wrong with the plan.

Emily poked her in the ribs. "What do you have for lunch today?"

Eying the clock above the chalkboard, Lizzie whispered, "It's 9:30 in the morning. How come you're thinking about lunch?"

"We're supposed to be looking at our complex-carbohydrates intake today," Emily said, glancing at the teacher, who had begun writing the assignment on the board. "You look like you're in spaceland."

Lizzie shrugged. "I got a bunch of things on my mind, like Trevor."

"Oh." Emily nodded. Lizzie had told her about the letter, and Emily had said the plan was ingenious. "Did he get the letter?"

Tight-lipped, Ms. Borlino shot Emily a look from across the room, so the letter discussion had to wait until recess.

Trevor had got the letter from Andrew Long. He was waving it in the air as the kids huddled around him at recess. They were standing in the Back 50, a large area near the back fence in the playground, far back from the school and away from the prying eyes of teachers on yard duty. It was the place to go to talk privately or to have snow wars without getting caught; some of the older kids snuck behind the pine trees to smoke, and the teachers couldn't see a thing.

Joy Lynn Goddard

Emily, Alex and Lizzie clumped through the snow to the Back 50 and joined the huddle of kids. Trevor, in the centre, was bragging, with his chest puffed out so much that his jacket wasn't staying closed. "That night I played the best game ever. It was touch and go until the third period, but then we got 'em. I got two goals!"

Willy's mouth dropped open, "Lemieux's cousin must have seen that game!"

"You're lucky," Sean shouted above the wind that was swirling snow in the circle of faces.

"Do you think the letter's for real?" Adam asked cautiously.

Alex and Lizzie exchanged looks, speaking only with their eyes and trying desperately not to laugh.

"What?" Sean moved closer to Adam. "Of course it's for real."

Hunching into his coat, Adam looked away. "I just wondered . . ."

"It's real," Nicole piped up. "I'm pretty sure I've heard of Andrew Long. My brother's got a book on

DAREDEVILS

Lemieux. It says something about his cousin, and I think he's from Montreal, where Lemieux was born."

"Sounds real to me," Lisa said.

"Sure does," Emily added, lowering her eyes before giving herself away.

"Who's coming to the arena with me?" Trevor studied each face around the circle. "Today's the big day."

"The letter says you're not supposed to tell anyone," Willy said. "It might fall through."

"Ha, don't pay any attention to that," Trevor cried, pushing Willy backwards. "Just stay out of the scout's way and don't ask him to get Lemieux to sponsor you too."

Everybody wanted to see the letter again, so when the bell rang, they were all late getting back to class. Ms. Borlino glared at them as they trouped in silently, hung up their coats, and kicked off their boots in a slushy row at the back of the room.

"What took you so long?" With her hands on her hips, Ms. Borlino meant business.

Nobody said a word.

"We had a good reason," Sean spoke up, turning to Trevor.

"Tell her, Trevor." Lisa batted her eyes.

"Um, we had to talk about this," Trevor said, handing his teacher the letter and holding back a grin. "Mario Lemieux's going to sponsor me. It's all there on paper."

Examining the letter, Ms. Borlino frowned. "This sounds really exciting, Trevor. But be careful that this is an authentic letter from Mr. Long. Did you show your parents?"

"No." He shook his head. "I just got the letter this morning, after they'd gone to work. I'm gonna surprise them after I talk with Lemieux's cousin."

"Well, I'd check it out with your parents first," she said, handing back the letter. "You shouldn't meet strangers on your own. It's not safe."

Nodding, Trevor sat down.

At her desk, Lizzie leaned closer to Emily and whispered, "Ms. Borlino has blown everything. Now Trevor's gonna tell his parents and they'll think something's pretty weird. They won't let him go in a million years."

Emily eyeballed Trevor and hissed, "I wouldn't worry – Trevor never listens to Ms. Borlino or anybody else. He'll go."

When Lizzie and Emily arrived at the arena, it was 4:15 p.m. They sat in the dark blue wooden stands and peered over the Plexiglass rimming the ice at a group of young children taking skating lessons. The children were skating on the sides of their skates, holding on to chairs for balance; Lizzie remembered skating like that, years ago, when she was just learning to skate. After a few tries, she hadn't needed the chair, and she'd loved getting on the ice every chance she got. She still felt that way.

Alex pushed through the double doors to the stands, and Lizzie and Emily waved him over. Hopping over a barrier, he took a seat. "I just saw Nicole and Lisa," he said. "They're at the concession booth."

Emily leaned forward, stretching to see across the rink. "And here comes Mary and Jennifer. There's Willy and Adam, too."

"I bet the whole class shows up," said Alex, jumping to his feet.

He can't sit still, Lizzie thought, watching him climb to the top of the stands and pick his way across, like a sure-footed cat. It was torture for him to sit through class each day; he was constantly asking to go to the bathroom or to wipe the boards or run errands, anything to get out of his seat. Craning her neck, she called up to him, "See anyone else yet?"

"Yup, here comes Sean and Trevor."

Most of Ms. Borlino's class showed up at the rink and they all sat together. It was 4:30 p.m. Trevor looked up from his watch to scan the faces in the arena.

"It's still early," Sean said. "He'll be here soon."

"I bet Andrew Long looks just like Lemieux," Willy said.

"Hard to tell, he could look like anybody," Sean said, standing up and searching the stands. "Maybe he's here, right this minute, but doesn't want to come over because of the crowd."

"That's right." Willy eyed Trevor. "The letter said you weren't supposed to tell anyone."

"I'll sit close but away from everybody," Trevor announced, his eyes flitting towards the players' box. "He'll see me better there."

Twenty long minutes passed. Trevor fidgeted with the zipper on his coat, took his hat off, put it on again, and then he took it off. A stranger approached but walked right past Trevor towards a little girl waving at the man from the ice. The skating lesson ended and another began, this time with older kids.

"He's not gonna show," Willy sighed.

"Maybe he's in another spot in the building and doesn't know Trevor's here," Sean said.

"I've got a great idea." Nicole jumped up and started climbing down the stands. "I'll get the manager to make an announcement over the P.A." She headed through the doors to the front office. Soon the kids heard the crackle of the P.A. followed by a booming voice which summoned: *"Andrew Long,*

Joy Lynn Goddard

please report to the players' box immediately. I repeat, Andrew Long."

Trevor's head jerked up. He searched the doors, and when no one appeared, his face turned redder by the minute.

Another ten minutes passed. Tired of waiting, kids began squirming in their seats. Lisa started throwing popcorn onto the ice, one piece at a time. Nicole scratched her name in the dark blue stands with a pen. A caretaker picked up a candy wrapper that Mary had thrown out and walked towards the children, scowling. "What are you kids doing here? Can't you read the sign?" He jabbed a finger towards the wall above the stands. "It says no loitering."

"We're just waiting for someone. He's coming soon," Willy said.

"Wait somewhere else," he grumbled, walking away, a large green bag of garbage swinging from his belt.

"Come on everybody," Willy jumped up. "He's not gonna show. This must be some kind of a joke." He shot Trevor a dirty look.

DAREDEVILS

"Right," Adam said, eyeballing Trevor and standing up, "I *thought* the letter was a fake. I'm not staying one more second."

"Wait a minute," Sean said quickly. "Trevor wouldn't set *himself* up. Think about it." Turning to the players' box, he waved his best friend over. "He'll tell you."

Nudging Alex, Lizzie whispered, "I think it's time for the grand finale." They'd been working on it for days – getting the plan just right. Climbing down from the stands, Lizzie and Alex hurried over to Sean and Trevor. Turning to face the other kids, Lizzie waved her arms in the air and shouted to get everyone's attention, "Hey – Andrew Long is right here. He's in the building."

"That's right." Alex nodded and took a deep breath.

"What? Where?" The kids, all talking at once, looked around the arena and then stared at Lizzie and Alex with eyes bugging out.

Alex turned to Trevor. In his deepest voice – the one he'd worked on until Lizzie had said that it sounded like it was coming from the bottom of his boots – he announced, "I'm Andrew Long." And with a smirk, he stuck out his hand and shook Trevor's. "It's a pleasure to meet the world's next Super Mario, or should I say, *Super Trevor*."

Trevor was speechless, his mouth open and his face bright red.

CHAPTER 9
THE BAD LUCK BLUES

Lizzie ate toast with peanut butter almost every morning; she liked the crunchy kind, the jar with the whole peanut on top, and always spread it so thickly that she had a hard time getting it down her throat without a class of milk. This morning, however, she had hardly taken a bite before pushing the plate of toast across the dining room table. She didn't feel right; something was wrong in the house. Her mother hadn't come downstairs yet, although she was usually the first one to get up, and Lizzie had heard her mother crying the night before.

Leaning back in the chair, her arms crossed, Lizzie gazed at the angel on the shelf across the room, the Christmas angel that was kept out all year round. She wished with all her heart that the angel could work some miracle and turn her string of bad luck into good. She'd had nothing but bad luck all month. February was always full of bad luck.

Last February she'd had an accident when tobogganing on the hill behind the arena. Freezing rain had pelted the hill for days, making it a slick, icy slope. It had been so slippery that kids could slide down the hill without toboggans. But those who wanted to go extra fast had used toboggans. Lizzie had been one of them. She didn't remember the accident; just getting on the front of her toboggan with Emily in back and waking up on the ground with a pounding headache; she also recalled a bunch of kids standing over her making a big fuss and her trip to the hospital. She'd had a concussion.

This February things weren't much better. On Pizza Day, last Thursday, somebody had stolen her money and she couldn't buy a piece of pepperoni pizza with the rest of the class, and since she hadn't brought a lunch from home, her stomach grumbled all afternoon. But far worse, was the day St. Mark's participated in the Kiwanis Music Festival. Remembering, Lizzie blushed.

DAREDEVILS

The Festival was a big event for St. Mark's School. Every year the school choir competed against choirs from all over the county, all hoping for top prizes. Trying to impress the judges, the teachers made the kids stand like statues, with feet exactly 20 centimetres apart and backs so straight that the kids could probably balance books on their heads. Once on stage, the kids couldn't laugh, whisper or slouch. Also in hopes of leaving a good impression, the boys wore crisp white shirts and dark pants; the girls wore snow-white blouses with dark skirts. Lizzie hated skirts. Fortunately, it was pretty cold in Northview most of the year and she could wear pants most of the time. She had only one skirt in her closet – a denim wraparound – and she wore it to the festival.

When it was St. Mark's turn to perform, the kids stood up without a sound – they'd been warned not to make a peep or they'd be in big trouble – and they followed one behind the other to the front of the crowded music hall. Squeezing between the front row of seats and the piano and music stand, the choir reached the stage, a low wooden platform across the front of the hall. Following in line, Lizzie felt a tug at the waistband of her skirt. The tie that hung from her waistband was snagged in the music stand.

She yanked at the tie but it tangled further. As she tugged a second time, her skirt fell off. There she stood, in front of the audience, in white underwear and her first pair of pantyhose.

There was dead silence.

In a panic, she pulled at the skirt-tie, but it still held fast in the stand.

The piano player jumped up to help. Seconds seemed like minutes and minutes like hours as the woman tried to free the skirt. Lizzie's mother, chalk-white, ran over to help, and the two women managed to free the skirt and wrap it around Lizzie.

Lizzie, her cheeks burning, her snow-white blouse limp from sweat, stood as if glued to the floor, with a hall full of people watching her. She wished with all her might that the floor would open up and swallow her, or that she could flee from the room and hide, but she stayed, afraid to call further attention to herself.

With wooden legs, she climbed onto the stage and stood with the others.

The kids in her choir gawked at her, whispering, some laughed openly, until the choir teacher sent them all a withering look and smiled sympathetically at Lizzie, and then they got ready to sing. The teacher nodded to the piano player, and the first bars of the song rang throughout the hall.

As her classmates sang, the song stuck in Lizzie's throat like peanut butter.

Lizzie wiped toast crumbs from the dining room table and took her plate and empty glass to the sink. Opening the fridge door, she searched for the lunch that her mother had made the night before, a tuna sandwich and some cookies, and stuck the lunch in her bookbag, along with a banana. Laura still hadn't come downstairs. The shower was running from the tenant's apartment in the basement, but there was only silence from the bathroom upstairs and from her mother's bedroom. Lizzie assumed that her mother was

Joy Lynn Goddard

sleeping late because she hadn't got much sleep the night before.

The trouble had started yesterday, after school. Tara, who had been invited for dinner, was on the phone in the family room when Lizzie walked in to watch television. She didn't notice Lizzie. Stretched out on the couch with her back to the door, she was reading something to someone on the other end of the phone. Lizzie didn't pay much attention until she heard Tara making fun of the familiar words:

"After I've finished playing in the NHL, I'm going to coach. I'll coach the Leafs and we'll win the Stanley Cup – the first victory in years."

Tara, falling back on the cushions, laughed so long and hard that tears ran down her cheeks. On her lap was Lizzie's class project, an autobiography about her hopes and dreams. After spending a month writing it, Lizzie had taken great pride in drawing a tiger on the cover, representing a hockey career that got started with the Tigers in Northview. The project was much too personal to be read by anyone but her teacher and Lizzie's best friend, Emily. Lizzie had locked it in her desk with plans to keep it there for many, many years, until the day she would show it to her own children.

It was obvious that Tara had been nosing around in Lizzie's room, had found the key under the plant pot, had unlocked the secret drawer in the desk and discovered the autobiography.

Lizzie marched over to the couch and snatched the project from Tara's lap. "How dare you! Keep your paws off my personal stuff. You had no right to go into my desk!"

Tara's mouth fell open. "Gotta go, Phil," she whispered in the phone. "The Lizard's back."

"And my name's not Lizard," Lizzie fumed, digging her hands in her hips. "It's Lizzie or Elizabeth. Pick one."

Tara scrambled off the couch and ran from the room like a jackrabbit.

The racket brought Lizzie's mother to the room. Blurting out the whole story, Lizzie was afraid that Laura would be furious with her for not trying harder to get along with Tara; but instead, her mother said next to nothing, gave her a big hug and then hurried out of the room. It was strange.

The first thing Lizzie did was pick up the phone and call Alex. He'd become a really good friend – ever since the day he'd helped get even with Trevor. Trevor hadn't said one creepy thing to Lizzie or Alex for weeks, or set foot near them. Although she was glad that he'd got what he deserved, she couldn't help feeling a little sorry for him. After all, he had looked like a great big jerk in front of the whole class.

She was still talking to Alex when her mother returned to the family room to use the phone. Lizzie left the room, closing the door, but she still heard most of her mother's conversation; it wasn't hard: her sweet, quiet mother was gone, replaced by a shrieking crazy woman. It was very clear that Laura was talking to Pete, and the subject was Tara. Lizzie had seen this crazy woman only one time before, and that was after a reckless driver had almost hit Lizzie with his car.

After she hung up, Laura sailed out of the room without a word and shut herself in her bedroom for the evening.

The next morning she came downstairs much later than usual; Lizzie had already finished breakfast, had put her dishes in the dishwasher and had packed her books in her bookbag by the time her mother appeared. She made herself a coffee, but no breakfast, and sat at the dining room table staring into her cup, saying nothing for the longest time. Then, with eyes red-rimmed and puffy, she glanced up at Lizzie who was ready to go out the door. "Ah, just thought you should know."

Lizzie's heart jumped. Here it comes, she thought, but she didn't know what. Bracing herself, she asked. "What's wrong?"

Laura swallowed hard. "Well, Pete and I thought that we'd better put the wedding plans on hold."

Tara, skunk hair, blue nails, and big mouth, immediately sprang to mind. Her move into the Lockyers' house would be delayed for a long time to come, and Lizzie felt like dancing, until she spotted the tear trickling down her mother's face.

"Actually, we'll probably call off the wedding altogether," Laura said.

Joy Lynn Goddard

Lizzie caught her breath. "No, don't do that. "It's because of me and Tara isn't it?"

"Hmm . . . It's a number of things, really." Her mother's voice was very soft and raspy with tears. With slow, circular motions, she rubbed her temples and then looked pointedly at her daughter. "Don't blame yourself."

"But," Lizzie said, moving closer. "You can't . . ."

"End of discussion." Laura looked away, her jaw tight, and Lizzie knew that her mother had said all she was going to say on the subject.

With a heavy heart, Lizzie pulled on her boots and stomped down the front porch into the chilly February morning.

CHAPTER 10
IN LIKE A LION, OUT LIKE A LAMB

Lizzie snuggled deep under her covers and tried to stifle the radio announcer's bright voice as it woke her from a sound sleep. "Good morning, people. It's Friday morning, the first day of March."

Groaning, she curled herself up into a ball to keep warm. Despite the thick wool socks that she always wore to bed in the winter, her toes were like blocks of ice. Her bedroom was often so cold that she could actually see her breath. The furnace didn't pipe enough hot air from the basement, which according to the tenant, was always nice and toasty.

The announcer broke into her thoughts. "The weather looks blustery today, but take heart, folks – remember the old saying: *If March comes in like a lion, it will go out like a lamb.*"

Hearing the word *lion* twigged a memory and she bolted upright in bed, banging her head on the wooden headboard. "The Lions. We're playing the Lions tonight."

She threw off her covers and snatched her housecoat on her way to the window. A thin stream of light was cutting through the gray morning. She hoped a storm wasn't coming. That meant the buses would be cancelled, and the Northview Tigers wouldn't be playing the London Lions in Niagara Falls that night. All winter she'd been looking forward to the finals.

After pouring boiling water into a bowl of instant oatmeal, Lizzie stirred the cereal furiously, as if quick action would somehow speed up the day and bring on the night. She gulped down the oatmeal, threw on her coat and headed to Emily's house. Most mornings the girls walked to school together, and sometimes Alex met up with them along the way.

Emily used to say that Alex was the weirdest kid in the school and that she wouldn't be caught dead with him, but now she didn't seem to mind when he tagged along with her and Lizzie – ever since that day in the arena when "Andrew Long" showed up and made a fool out of Trevor.

Lizzie was glad that she had both Alex and Emily as friends. Sometimes she told Emily things that she couldn't tell Alex, and at other times she told Alex things that she couldn't tell Emily. She talked about hockey with Alex, arguing that her favourite team, the Leafs, was much better than his favourite team, the Canadiens, and with Emily she talked her heart out about personal stuff. She told Emily that Pete was no longer coming around the house and that Laura had called off the wedding.

"Least you don't have to put up with Tara anymore," Emily had pointed out. "Beats me how you put up with old 'skunk hair' this long."

As Emily and Lizzie approached Alex at the intersection, his head was down, and he seemed unaware of the traffic whizzing past. Just as a car was speeding towards him, he took a step from the curb.

"Alex!" Lizzie cried, and he stepped back onto the sidewalk, his face blank. After the light turned green, the girls ran up to him.

"You almost got killed!" Emily's eyes bugged out. "You could have been a statistic in tomorrow's newspaper. Didn't you see the car?"

Joy Lynn Goddard

With a shrug, Alex gazed down the street where the car had long gone. He turned back to the girls. "I guess my mind's on other things."

"What things?" Emily asked, scrunching up her face. "What's more important than staying alive?"

Alex kicked a chunk of ice down the sidewalk. "What's that?"

Taking a step closer, Emily stuck her face into Alex's until their noses were practically touching. "Earth to Alex. What's on your mind?"

"Is it tonight's game?" Lizzie jumped in.

"Well, we've got a really good chance at the title," he said, frowning. "I don't want to blow it or anything."

Lizzie stuck out her chin. "Alex Fabiano, you're one of the best players on the team. Coach Powers said so. I heard him, and that's a fact."

"Really?" His eyes lit up.

"Yup." Lizzie said, nodding.

A grin spread across his face. "He thinks you're pretty good too."

Emily groaned. "If you guys are finished with all the gooey stuff, I just heard the bell. Come on. We're going to be late."

The morning was long, and the afternoon seemed even longer. Lizzie tried to concentrate on the assignment – drawing African animals for the front foyer – but she had a really hard time, even though she liked art class almost as much as gym class. Her mind kept wandering to the weekend tournament in Niagara Falls; the Northview Tigers were going to play the London Lions, the North Lake Hawks and the Niagara Falls Wolves.

She flipped through several animal books in the library, searching for just the right picture to copy. She wanted to draw the tiger, of course. There were pictures of passive tigers stretched out sleepily in the grassland under a blazing sun, and there were pictures of aggressive beasts, baring jagged teeth and ready to pounce. Lizzie stopped at a picture of a full-grown tiger standing on a large rock, watching for movement

Joy Lynn Goddard

in the tall, parched grasses below. This was the picture that she decided to draw.

In the back of her mind, she heard Coach Powers telling the team to be as aggressive as a tiger, to be ready for every move made by the opponent; the tiger is aggressive for a reason – to survive in the wild. He was always encouraging the team to be aggressive for a reason too – to defend the net and win the game. He wouldn't put up with aggressive behaviour with no purpose behind it – like the behaviour that landed Sean and Trevor in the penalty box again and again.

The wind had died down by late afternoon, and the snow that had fallen all day now lay thick on the streets, the colour of mud from car exhaust. Gray clouds blanketed the city, threatening to dump more snow. With hopes that the bad weather would hold off until the bus made it to Niagara Falls, the Tigers quickly got ready to leave.

The bus pulled up in front of Northview Community Centre. Trevor was on first, laying claim to a back seat and making room for Sean.

DAREDEVILS

Journeys away from home were sometimes hard for the only girl on a boys' hockey team. Sleeping arrangements could be a problem. Each hotel room was to be shared by four players, all boys. Lizzie usually bunked with her mother, but since her mother couldn't get away until the next day, she'd be sleeping in the hotel room alone that night, with the coach's wife looking in on her. She wished for the hundredth time that Northview had Rep teams, not just House League teams, for girls, but the city was small, and there wasn't much interest in girls' hockey yet.

She climbed on the bus and scanned the sea of faces, which were all laughing and talking and kidding around. As usual, all the boys ignored her, except Alex. Sitting halfway down the aisle in a seat by himself, he waved her over.

At the back of the bus, Trevor and Sean got louder and louder as they played the *Double Dare Game*. The whole bus could hear them daring each other to do silly pranks, and Lizzie hoped that the boys would leave her and Alex alone. They stayed clear of her and Alex most of the time now.

Joy Lynn Goddard

Then she heard Trevor chant:

> *Double dare,*
> *Double dare,*
> *Take the hat off*
> *Lizzie's hair.*

The bus was just heading south, out of Northview, when Sean pounced on Lizzie and snatched her hat away. Trevor's nasty laugh travelled from the back of the bus, making the hairs on the back of Lizzie's neck stand on end. "Looks like little Lizzie is having a bad hair day," he cried.

Lizzie swung around and made a face at him as Coach Powers bellowed from the front of the bus, "Settle down back there. It's going to be a long ride. Save your energy for the Lions tonight. And Sean, give the hat back."

With a groan, he tossed the hat back to Lizzie, and she quickly pulled it on. Then sliding down in her seat, she prayed the attention would soon turn to someone else. If it didn't, it would be a long trip.

For most of the trip, the hum of the engine and the murmur of voices were the only noises heard on the bus until, from a back seat, Trevor began to chant:

> *Double dare,*
> *Double dare,*
> *Kiss Lizzie, Alex,*
> *If you care.*

The bus fell silent. All eyes were turned on Alex and Lizzie. From her chest and neck, heat rose steadily into her face. She was certain that she looked like a bright red tomato. Fixing her eyes on the seat in front, Lizzie shut out everyone, especially Trevor.

Then she stole a look at Alex; he was red too.

Lowering his head, he muttered, "Creep."

"Yah, jerk. Big fat jerk."

Trevor wouldn't quit:

> *K-I-S-S-I-N-G,*
> *Lizzie and Alex*
> *Sitting in a tree,*

Joy Lynn Goddard

> *First comes love,*
> *Then comes marriage,*
> *Then comes Lizzie*
> *With a baby carriage.*

Lizzie scrunched down farther in her seat. "Just ignore him," she told Alex. Knowing Trevor, she thought, he'd stop if he didn't have an audience. At school he'd often talk and fool around a lot, but he usually stopped if no one was looking at him.

Leaning closer to Alex, she whispered, "Trevor's gonna quit if he hasn't got your attention, you'll see." No sooner were the words out of her mouth then she got the strangest feeling that Trevor was never going to quit. Although his attention had turned to the glittery lights of Niagara Falls, as the bus entered the main street, she felt certain that Trevor would be back – big mouth and all.

CHAPTER 11
DAREDEVILS

The Niagara Falls Wolves' Number 9 had become an even better player since the last time his team had played the Tigers. He was tall, at least a head taller than the other players on his team, and he had broad shoulders, like a man's, and because of his size, he seemed to take over the ice; he was fast as well, as fast as a flying puck. Lizzie's stomach flipped over every time Number 9 raced towards the net. He swooped in front of Willy, the Tigers' Number 4, and then with steely determination he zoomed past Alex. Lizzie leapt at the puck and blocked it with the flat of her hockey stick, a smack heard throughout the arena.

Jumping out of their seats, the spectators roared their applause. Lizzie took a deep breath and smiled up into the stands, hoping to see her mother who had arrived earlier in the day, but Lizzie couldn't find her amid the sea of screaming faces.

This was the Tigers' second game of the day. They'd won their first game against the North Lake

Hawks and had beaten the London Lions the night before. If they beat the Wolves, they'd be very close to winning the championship game on Sunday and taking home the gleaming silver-plated trophy. The trophy shimmered in its brightly lit glass case, which was just inside the front door of the Niagara Falls arena. Lizzie had examined every centimetre of the trophy earlier, noticing each date and team that had won the trophy. The Tigers had won it only once before, four years ago.

It was two minutes before the end of the third period. The score was tied, 1-1. Lizzie felt hot and sweaty, her hair sticking to the inside of her helmet, yet she could see her breath coming out in short puffs in the frosty rink.

When her team raced the puck to the other end, she let down her guard with a sigh of relief. The Tigers' centre passed the puck to Alex, who was on left wing, and then Alex took control of the action. Skating fiercely, he plowed through the other players. A top scorer and faster than all his teammates, he seemed to have more ice time than anyone else now, thought Lizzie with satisfaction.

Scooping up the puck, he shot hard. The Wolves' goalie lunged but just missed the puck, and it slammed into the net. Shouting joyfully, the Tigers threw up their hands and swooped towards Alex as the crowd roared from the stands.

Shortly thereafter, the buzzer announced the end of the game and Lizzie leapt towards her knot of teammates. The Tigers had won 2-1.

In the dressing room the excitement continued with the Tigers whooping it up. They had earned a spot in the championship game and now had a chance to take the trophy home. Alex was their hero. He'd scored both goals against the Wolves. Rallying around him, the players shoved him around playfully. Lizzie was so proud of him. Until recently, he'd had no friends, except Emily and Lizzie. Now he was Mr. Popular, and the Tigers respected him, all except Trevor and Sean. While the others were huddling around Alex, Trevor and Sean stood back along the benches and said nothing; they went about their business, stuffing

Joy Lynn Goddard

hockey gear into their bags and wiping off their skate blades.

Since all games were finished for the day, the Tigers celebrated with pizza and Coke and then climbed on the bus to visit some of the local tourist attractions in the city.

They stopped first at a wax museum, a small, dingy building that was sandwiched between two taller buildings on the main street. A solitary light shone at the front door. It was dark and cool inside, with a dusty and musty smell. All voices hushed in wonder. Lizzie shivered when she spied the first lifelike wax body in a corner by the door. Its black cape swept the ground. In a pale, sickly face, its long, jagged teeth were yellow with age, and its lips were blood red. A vampire. Lizzie swallowed hard.

The narrow hall was long and winding. Glass cubicles ran along its length. Inside each were wax people from all different backgrounds and time periods, some famous, some not so famous. There was Queen Elizabeth, draped in a long blue gown, sitting on her throne with a crown shining on top of her head. There was Hitler, the German dictator who was responsible for the deaths of millions of people during World War 11, a small wax figure dressed in a brownish-gray military uniform, staring proudly into the distance, his mouth set determinedly under a small black mustache.

"Hey, Lizzie, come here," Alex kept his voice low. "Look at him." He tapped on the glass of a cubicle.

Lizzie peered inside. In front of a mural of Niagara Falls, a blond figure was perched on a high wire, balancing with a long wooden pole.

"It's Blondin," Alex piped up. "Remember, we read about him in school?"

"Blondin?" Spreading her hands on the windowpane, Lizzie leaned closer to take a better look. "Oh, that guy." She stepped back. "He's the one who crossed Niagara Falls on a tightrope."

"He crossed at least a hundred times!" Alex's eyes lit up.

"Oh, that's right. And he never fell, not once."

"He even crossed with someone on his back!"

Joy Lynn Goddard

Lizzie turned to Alex, her arms crossed. "He must have been pretty crazy to do that."

He shrugged. "I tried that once."

"You what?"

"I mean, I tried walking across a tightrope in my backyard. I was kind of playing circus. I tied the rope to two trees and I got a broom to help me balance. It was cool."

"Did you fall off?"

He snickered. "A whole bunch of times. But I got the knack of it once I got rid of my shoes."

"You wouldn't catch me doing that in a million years," Lizzie said, shaking her head. "I don't like heights. Come on." She tugged Alex's sleeve. "Let's catch up with the others."

As the team travelled to Horseshoe Falls, Lizzie's thoughts drifted to her first time there, with her classmates last June. The kids had explored long winding tunnels which led to lookouts over the river and to a platform near the brink of the falls. Before going underground, they'd put on shiny yellow slickers and black boots, with hopes of protecting themselves from the spray, but they'd got soaked anyway. Lizzie remembered looking through an opening in the rock face, awe-struck: The falls pounded the river, creating a billowy mist that rose over rocks and water and almost hid the tour boat, *The Maid of the Mist*, as it chugged along the river.

Night had fallen and clusters of twinkling lights illuminated an icy wonderland. Winter had frozen the trees into various poses. The river was partially frozen. Huge chunks of ice moved slowly along with the force of the falls.

"Wow!" Alex jumped off the bus and ran through throngs of tourists towards the Niagara Gorge. Lizzie and her mother followed close behind him and joined him at the railing.

Lights lit up walls of ice and jagged rock in the deep and wide gorge. As water churned the river, a mist rose, like clouds.

Gazing at the powerful falls, Lizzie's mother sighed softly. "It never ceases to take my breath away. And I've been here at least a dozen times."

Joy Lynn Goddard

Lizzie clutched the metal railing and gaped downward to the bottom of the gorge, her stomach dropping, like riding in an elevator.

Along the railing, the Tigers, wearing bright orange hockey jackets, were hard to miss. Sean pitched something over the edge and the boys leaned over the railing to watch it fall. Legs wobbling, Lizzie stepped back.

The horizontal bars of the railing were anchored in a cement base. Alex grabbed hold of the top bar and swung his body up, then sat on the base, dangling his legs into the gorge. Mesmerized by the rising mist, he seemed lost in his own world.

"Alex, get down." Just watching him, Lizzie felt queasy. "You're gonna fall."

"No, I'm okay," Alex said, gripping the railing tighter. "Don't worry."

Nearby, Trevor, Willy and Sean were fooling around. Sean was standing on the cement base, with the top bar of the railing barely reaching his thighs. With his arms outstretched for balance, he took a few steps and then jumped down and landed on the sidewalk.

"Who's next?" He eyeballed Willy. "How about you?"

Backing away from the railing, Willy shook his head. "No way. Think I'm nuts?"

"Where's the next daredevil?" Trevor looked around and spied Alex. "Got any guts?"

Lizzie looked for help. Her mother was deep in conversation with Coach Powers and his wife, too far along the sidewalk to be of much help, so Lizzie took matters into her own hands. Moving closer to Alex, she pleaded, "Ignore him. He'll go away, you'll see."

Alex squinted at her briefly and turned back to the gorge. "It won't make any difference. You know Trevor."

"Don't be crazy!" Lizzie swallowed hard, her heart thumping so loudly she was certain all the kids along the railing could hear it. The cement was icy and too narrow to walk on safely. "Don't do it." She tugged the sleeve of his jacket. "You'll fall."

Joy Lynn Goddard

With his eyes fixed on the churning water below, Alex was silent.

Trevor began to chant:

> *Double Dare,*
> *Double Dare,*
> *Show us that you*
> *Have no care.*

Alex pulled himself up on the cement base. Grasping the top bar to steady himself, he turned sideways, and then he let go, with the railing not quite as high as his waist. Like Blondin perching on a high wire, Alex spread his arms for balance and took a few tentative steps. Lizzie forced herself to breathe, telling herself that Alex was a sure-footed cat, picking its way across a high, narrow ledge.

But Alex lost his balance. It happened so fast. Slipping on a patch of ice, he swung his arms frantically through sky and mist, in hopes of grabbing the railing, but it was too low – and so there was nothing to break his fall.

Lizzie gasped, her mouth frozen open in terror as Alex toppled over the railing headfirst, his bright orange hockey jacket a neon ball plunging through the sky. The ball smashed into jagged rock and continued its descent, then was swallowed by the mist.

Breaking the eerie silence, Lizzie let out a bone-chilling cry.

When her mother, the coach and his wife, along with what seemed like a hundred other people rushed to her side, Lizzie couldn't speak. She hung on the railing so desperately that her knuckles were white and then peered into the gorge, her head spinning and her stomach threatening to bring up her dinner. Pointing down to where her friend had disappeared in the darkness, she shrieked, "Alex!"

Her chest tight, she couldn't breathe. Tears spilled down her cheeks. It seemed like everyone was crying. Coach Powers began barking orders for someone to call rescue workers and for his team to back away from the railing and stay together.

It seemed like hours before Lizzie heard the wail of sirens and watched as a frenzy of police cars and other emergency vehicles screeched to a halt in front of her, but it was only minutes. She told her story to the many rescue workers, how Alex had fallen, where he had fallen and what she'd seen from beginning to end, and after she'd finished, limp and still crying, her mother attempted to steer her away from the crowds. But Lizzie refused to budge. Pulling herself together, she wiped her tears, determined to help.

At the railing, a police officer surveyed the gorge and then walked over to a firefighter nearby. "It's next to impossible. The gorge is too wide, too deep. It's like looking for a needle in a haystack."

The firefighter sighed heavily. "And the darkness doesn't help."

"There's too much mist," said the police officer, leaning closer to the firefighter. "Let's face it. Even if we do spot the boy, he probably didn't make it. In that case, is it worth risking our men to retrieve the body? We'd probably have more deaths on our hands."

Lizzie couldn't believe her ears. The men were giving up on Alex, and he was still alive! He had to be. Moving closer to the men, she strained to hear more.

The police officer was deep in thought, his hands on his hips and his head down, silent for a long time. Finally, turning to the firefighter, he said, "I have a young boy, and I'd want everything possible done if he were my son in that gorge. Maybe the boy's alive. Chances are slim, I know, but we have to try."

"We'll work our way up from the bottom," said the firefighter. "There are tunnels . . . We may spot him from an opening . . . We can lower a stretcher from the top and bring him up. If we can spot him, and that's a big *if*."

Lizzie had explored the tunnels on her last school trip. They led to lookouts in the rock face and to a platform jutting into the gorge. She could help. She knew the spot where Alex had fallen, and it wasn't far from the falls. Knowing her mother would never let her join a dangerous rescue, Lizzie kept her plans secret. While Laura was talking to Coach Powers, Lizzie slipped quietly away.

The main entrance to the tunnels was blocked off with a wooden barrier, closing it to visitors at this time of the year. The gap underneath was just large enough for Lizzie to crawl under and start her descent. Terrified of the unknown in the cold, dark passage, she forced herself to move onward, knowing she had to reach Alex as soon as possible. The faster she got to him, the faster he'd be rescued and the faster he'd get the medical help he needed.

All she could think about was helping Alex. A true friend, he'd helped her many times before. He'd stuck up for her when Sean and Trevor had made fun of her. He'd told the police that Trevor, not Lizzie, had broken the Christmas lights at the Gallinas' place. Best of all, he'd come up with a great plan to put Trevor in his place by writing the "hockey scout" letter.

Sliding her hands along the icy rock wall, she crept along the tunnel blindly, the blackness as thick as fog. There was little air in the tunnel, and Lizzie couldn't tell how long or wide it was. She picked her feet over ice and rock until the ground suddenly disappeared.

Tumbling down an incline, she bashed her legs, arms and back, and then at a bend in the tunnel, her fall was broken by a barrier of jagged rock. The sound from her fall was deafening as it echoed off the walls of the tunnel. Her arm hurt and she rubbed it gently. Her back ached. Since she seemed to be able to move everything, she assumed that nothing was broken.

She limped forward along the tunnel, drawn towards a light that was sweeping in front of an opening in the rock face; search lights were illuminating rocks and mist and ice. Lizzie crawled up in the opening and then beyond, deeper into the gorge, until she found a ledge to sit on. Her legs dangling in midair, her hair and clothing soaked from spray, she held on to the rock ledge for dear life while she searched the black hole for her friend.

She was hypnotized by the swirling mist. Along the side where Alex had fallen, the mist seemed to take on a life of its own, puffy and white and shaped, curiously, like angel wings. The angel on the shelf at home sprang to mind, its white lace tattered, its halo askew from much handling; it seemed to watch over

Lizzie and Laura all year long. Thoughts of the angel brought comfort to Lizzie now, helping her feel somewhat safe despite the danger all around.

She heard a sound, a soft moan. Was it the wind?

"Alex!" Lizzie shouted into the blackness and mist. "Where are you?"

There was no sound but that of the pounding falls.

The angel wings lifted just as the search light swept the gorge – and Lizzie saw a spot of orange on a ledge in the rock face. Was it a Tigers jacket?

Mist moved in again and the spot of orange disappeared. Lizzie was certain that she could see the ledge where Alex had fallen, but she knew she couldn't reach it safely. It was too dark, and the rock face was too slippery.

"He's here, he's here," she cried out, hoping beyond reason to be heard. She didn't expect an answer. She wondered where the rescue workers were, if they'd gone another way in the tunnels, if they were still on their way. The roaring falls deadened any sounds of life.

DAREDEVILS

As the search lights continued to move across the area, an idea took shape in Lizzie's mind. Clinging to the rock face, she carefully climbed down to another ledge; then she unzipped her Tigers jacket and took it off. Bright orange, it would catch the light that was sweeping the gorge and draw attention like a beacon.

As the light fell in her direction, she waved the jacket over her head. But she wasn't sure that it could be seen. She must throw it high and farther into the gorge; she must get it as close as possible to the ledge that held Alex – just as the light was descending. With her heart pounding, she waited for the light. Bending forward, just short of the swirling mist below, she whipped her jacket in the air – and it glowed.

Her ears began to buzz. Just as she made it back through the opening in the tunnel, all went black.

CHAPTER 12
THE VISITORS

The pain woke Lizzie. Something was crushing her leg, and sharp pain was shooting up the right side of her body. On her side, she realized that her body weight was causing the problem. Rolling over, she opened her eyes to blackness. The sheets were scratchy and they smelled like antiseptic, not like the sheets on her bed at home, which smelled like the fabric softener that her mother always used in the washing machine.

Her arm felt tender, as if she'd been slammed into the net a few times, and she moved it carefully under the blanket until she felt more comfortable. Her mouth was as dry as soda crackers. "Water," she moaned.

A light clicked on by her bed and she adjusted to the brightness while someone brought a straw to her lips and she sipped from a glass of ice water. Looking up into the face of her mother, she tried to smile. Her mother's eyes, tired and red-rimmed, welled up with tears. "Thank God you're okay."

"Where am I?" She squinted at the crisp white blanket, the pale green walls and the empty metal bed, stripped of bedding, across the small room.

"You're in the hospital," Laura said. "Remember? We brought you here last night. You're going to be fine." Her eyes brightened.

Lizzie slowly propped herself up against the pillows, thinking. With her head throbbing, it was like thinking through fog, but some of what had happened the night before broke through. The cold, dark tunnel. The wail of sirens. The ambulance and stretcher.

"My leg hurts," she groaned.

"I'm not surprised. Your leg's broken, and you have some bruises and cuts too. You also have a slight concussion." Her mother drew in a breath and let it out slowly. "But the doctor says you're going to be fine."

The fog was lifting, and Lizzie's thoughts became crystal clear. The search lights. The thundering falls. Alex.

"Alex!" She sat up further in bed and stared at her mother, her heart racing. "Did they find Alex?"

Joy Lynn Goddard

Frowning, Laura reached over and picked up Lizzie's hand. "Yes, they did find Alex. Thanks to you. They saw your orange jacket, and they knew where to look. I don't know whether to yell at you or kiss you after running off like that." She squeezed Lizzie's hand. "That tunnel was so dangerous, and the gorge – you could have fallen too and . . ."

"Is he okay?"

Laura briefly shut her eyes. "We still don't know the full story. He was airlifted to a bigger hospital, and his parents are with him now. He was still in surgery when I phoned about an hour ago."

Swallowing the huge lump in her throat, Lizzie tried to speak – but nothing came out.

"There's hope," Laura said with false brightness. "The paramedics found him on a ledge about thirty metres into the gorge. It's amazing that he didn't fall off. The ledge wasn't very wide, just half a metre. There could have been more damage or he could have drowned. A miracle."

The angel wings – or mist – or whatever it was that Lizzie had seen when she was dangling from a ledge deep in the gorge, sprang to mind, and she sighed softly.

"What did he break?"

"Well, the doctors say he broke his jaw, several of his front teeth and his pelvis. Surprisingly, he had no head injuries. They think that when he fell headfirst, he struck his face on the wall of the gorge and that this impact turned him around, so he actually landed feetfirst on the ledge."

Alex was like a cat, thought Lizzie; it picked its way across a narrow path, fell, then usually landed on its feet. Alex, a cat with nine lives.

"How did they lift him out?"

"I didn't see everything. I just heard about it. I was busy with you. After the firefighters found you in the tunnel, unconscious, I rode with you in the ambulance to the hospital. I was told that the only way to get Alex out of the gorge was with a crane. Some type of cage with a stretcher was lowered and he was lifted out. Amazing." She shook her head slowly.

Light was beginning to filter through the thin curtains into the room as the sun rose over the sleeping city. The door swung open and a nurse walked in briskly with a tray of pills.

"Good morning, Elizabeth. You're looking better this morning. Glad to have you back with us." She smiled while handing her a tiny cup with pills, then refilling her water glass. "You must be a popular girl. We've been getting calls about you all night long."

"Oh?" Eyebrows raised, she glanced at her mother, then back at the nurse.

The nurse set down the tray and fished in her pocket, pulling out a slip of paper. "Let me see." She read the note. "Ricky, Willy, Adam and Sean called several times. Friends, I assume?"

Lizzie's mouth dropped open. "Not really. They're on my team, the Tigers, but most of the time they don't pay much attention to me."

"Well, they seemed pretty worried to me, especially Sean," the nurse said. "He's called every hour on the hour. The last time he phoned, we told him you were sleeping peacefully and he backed off a bit."

Sean, Trevor's best friend! Lizzie was speechless.

Laura rubbed her eyes and looked up wearily at the nurse. "Did the newspapers call again?"

"They did, Mrs. Lockyer. In fact, there's a reporter in the hall as we speak. I told him he had to wait until after breakfast before he could disturb you."

"You're a hero, you know." Laura turned to Lizzie. "You helped save Alex. You were the first one to spot him, and you led the rescue workers right to him."

A warm glow spread throughout Lizzie's body as if she'd sunk into a tub of warm, soapy water.

"It's all over the news," said the nurse, heading to the door and making way for an attendant who was pushing a cart into the room.

"Looks like breakfast has arrived," Laura said, nodding to the attendant, who left a tray next to the bed and then disappeared. "Hungry, Lizzie?"

"Kind of, but can we call the hospital about Alex first?"

Laura checked her watch. "It's still early. We'll call after breakfast, after you've spoken to the reporter."

Joy Lynn Goddard

Lizzie had never stayed in a hospital before. She'd gone to the emergency room – like the time she'd had a toboggan accident and ended up with a concussion – but she'd never spent the night. It was a treat to be fussed over and have food served in bed. She wanted to remember every detail so that she could tell Emily later.

Lifting the small square covers on the tray, she found cereal, eggs, toast and jam. The cereal was lumpy and cold, but it tasted good after she'd sprinkled it with a tablespoon of brown sugar. Her mother never let her put sugar on cereal at home, but she said nothing about it now and smiled. And she said nothing about the tea, which was steaming from a little metal pot on her tray, although Lizzie rarely drank tea at home.

Not long after she'd finished breakfast and had got ready for the day, the reporter was at the door. He was a thin, balding man who scurried into the room like a ferret. "Hello, little lady," he said, pulling up a chair with one hand while taking a notebook from his pocket with the other. "I hear you have quite a story to tell."

Lizzie began, slowly at first, trying to remember all the details of Alex's accident, and then when each terrifying moment came back, she spilled out the whole story, except for the part about the *Double Dare Game*; she didn't want to give the Tigers a bad name, any of them.

Her eyelids were getting heavy, for the pills she had taken to dull the pain were also making her very sleepy. The reporter must have noticed because he said, "Just a couple more questions and I'll let you rest." While flipping through his notebook he stopped to study a page. "Ah, here's my interview with your teammates, the Tigers. They said that Alex is one of the best players on the team. In fact, he was cleaning up at the tournament."

"Yup," Lizzie nodded, proud that the Tigers thought so highly of Alex. "He's the fastest player on the team."

"They also said that you're the best goalie in the tournament." He peered over the top of his glasses and grinned. "Now that you can't play, they think they're going to lose!"

Apparently, Alex's popularity was rubbing off on her, and she was struck speechless again.

"Guess you're a hero in more ways than one," he said, sticking his notebook in his pocket. Then he rose from the chair and headed to the door as quickly as he'd come in.

Thinking over his comments, Lizzie turned to her mother. "How come the Tigers seem to like me all of a sudden? They used to treat me like dirt."

As if searching for just the right answer, Laura stared blankly at the pale green wall across the room and then back, with eyes softer and dreamy – like they used to look when she was with Pete. "Well, sometimes people don't realize what they have until it's gone."

It struck Lizzie that her mother was not only talking about the Tigers, but she was also talking about herself and how much she missed Pete.

Then, surprisingly, as Lizzie was about to fall asleep from the pills she'd had earlier, there was a tap at the door and in wandered Pete.

Unshaven and eyes puffy, he was clutching a large potted plant that was shaped like a Christmas tree, with miniature yellow and orange bell-shaped peppers hanging from its branches. In awe, Lizzie gazed at the unusual plant, her mind drifting to the tree-trimming party with her mother's boyfriend and his daughter just a few months ago.

Laura sat up straight, and despite the dark circles under her eyes from a sleepless night, she appeared wide awake. Without saying a word, she followed Pete with her eyes as he walked towards the bed and set the gift on a nearby table.

"Thank you," Lizzie murmured.

Pete looked down at her and smiled, his blue eyes warm, crinkling at the corners. "I heard about the accident on the late news and thought you might need some cheering up. It's absolutely shocking about Alex. Is he . . .? Are you okay?" He stole a look at Laura. "I was so worried."

Suddenly Laura was up out of her chair and in Pete's arms. She stood there for what seemed like forever with tears rolling down her cheeks; and Lizzie couldn't tell if her mother was laughing or crying. Lizzie hadn't seen Pete in weeks and she'd missed him; it was obvious that her mother had too.

Pete broke away from Laura but still held her hand as he turned back to Lizzie. "How do you feel?"

"Okay." She shrugged. The pills had dulled the pain so she just felt sore. "I've got a broken leg." With her good arm, she threw off the covers to show him the cast. "See."

"I'm glad that's all that's broken," he said, leaning over the bed and hugging her. "You could've broken your neck or drowned! I'm so glad you're okay. How's Alex?"

"We're still waiting to find out," Laura's voice was soft and low. "No head injuries, though. He was in surgery the last time I talked to his parents."

Pete looked away briefly and then back, shaking his head. "It's simply unbelievable that he survived such a fall. He must have a guardian angel. Oh, and speaking of angels, I thought you might like to have one to help you recover, Lizzie." From out of his pocket, he pulled the angel from the dining room shelf.

DAREDEVILS

After adjusting its crooked halo and rumpled lace, he handed it to her.

Laura's eyes brightened. "How did you get it?"

"Oh, I have my ways," he chuckled. "Actually, I just went to your house and knocked. Your tenant let me in."

"I'm glad." Laura couldn't take her eyes off him.

"I hope you still feel that way when you see what else I brought along; I mean, who."

Laura and Lizzie exchanged looks.

"I'll be right back." Pete left the room and returned with Tara. "Skunk hair," Emily called her. But this time she wasn't sporting the skunk look, a yellow strip running down dark brown hair. Instead, her hair was red – all of it. Bright orange, actually. This time a carrot sprang to mind. Silently regarding Lizzie and Laura, Tara followed her dad into the room.

With an arm around his daughter, Pete pulled her closer and grinned. "This was the first time in years that I got Tara out of bed without a fight. As soon as she heard about Lizzie's accident, she was out of bed

Joy Lynn Goddard

like a shot. In fact, she got dressed and was in the car before me."

Tara took a step closer to the bed. "Hi, Lizard. How are ya?"

CHAPTER 13
THE FINAL GAME

Coach Powers came to the hospital to tell Lizzie the news that the Tigers, out of respect for their injured players, had decided to forfeit the championship game. They were far too upset to play after what had happened to Lizzie and Alex, and this meant that the Wolves would win the tournament by default.

The news brought mixed feelings – Lizzie was glad that the Tigers were thinking about her and Alex but disappointed that they'd miss the championship game. They had worked so hard, and now they had a really good chance to win the trophy. They shouldn't just throw it away.

The coach took a step from the bed, ready to leave.

"Wait," Lizzie said.

"Yes?" He raised his eyebrows.

"The Tigers have gotta play."

"But . . ."

"They've been dreaming about this game all season."

Joy Lynn Goddard

Coach Powers let out a heavy sigh, and then he grinned. "But we're missing our two best players."

Lizzie blushed. "Alex would *want* you to play. I know it."

His arms folded, Coach Powers gazed out the window for the longest time, as if deep in thought. "Okay. I'll tell the team." He leaned over and patted her shoulder. "You get some rest now," he said, and then he left. She was alone for the first time that day; Laura, Pete and Tara had gone to the hospital cafeteria to get something to eat, and then father and daughter were heading home to Northview.

Lizzie slid deep under the blanket and stared at the faint crack running across the pale green ceiling, her mind a kaleidoscope of changing colours and images: the Tigers at the championship game; Alex in a hospital bed, probably bandaged from head to toe; Laura and Pete together again; Tara, with hair like a carrot, being almost nice . . .

Pulling the scratchy sheets up to her chin, she tried to rest. The pain in her leg had deadened. The doctors had said that she needed to spend another night in the hospital just to be on the safe side. Her cast was heavy and clunky, and she had an itch deep down where it couldn't be reached. She wondered for the hundredth time about Alex's injuries.

Her mother had been phoning regularly for reports on his condition. His parents had said that the surgery had been successful, that Alex had awakened briefly but hadn't spoken before falling into a deep sleep again.

She got some rest before Pete and Tara stuck their heads in the room, just to say goodbye, and Laura pulled out a book and got comfortable in a chair by the bed.

There wasn't much to do in a hospital but stare at the walls or rest. A small television was suspended on a bracket above Lizzie's bed, but none of the programs interested her. Laura was helping Lizzie adjust the pillows when a loud honking from beneath the window caught their attention.

The honking got louder and more persistent, as if a horn was stuck or someone was sitting on it deliberately. Laura strode over to the window, darkened now with the night, except for a yellow glow from the street lamp directly below. "I think you'll want to see this," she said, glancing back with a knowing smile. It was the kind of smile she wore the day she pretended to have forgotten Lizzie's birthday, then handed her a present, the goalie stick Lizzie had wanted more than anything else in the world. Laura opened the latch and cracked the window, letting in the cool night air, and with it, another round of blasting from the horn, even louder now.

She drew back the covers on the bed and helped Lizzie to the window. A big yellow school bus was parked at the curb below, with kids poking their heads out the windows. The Tigers! Spotting Lizzie, they flung their arms up and waved enthusiastically, cheering at the top of their lungs. "You're the best!" a player shouted. "We lost 'cause you didn't play!" cried another.

Lizzie's disappointment over the team's loss quickly disappeared as it dawned on her how much the Tigers had missed her in the net. In its place was happiness that grew from deep inside and rose steadily, like a bubble. Catching her reflection in the windowpane, she was grinning from ear to ear. Lizzie waved at the Tigers, tears welling up in her eyes. At last she felt part of the team.

Weak from her injuries, she hobbled back to bed and was just climbing under the covers when Coach Powers, Willy and Sean wandered into the room.

Chuckling, the coach shot a look towards the window. "The nurses are having a fit with that racket outside. I guess we'd better get on our way soon. We just wanted to say goodbye before we left for home." He stood at the bottom of the bed beside Willy and Sean.

Leaning back against her pillows, Lizzie stared at her visitors, surprised by all the attention, especially from Sean. "Ah, I'm sorry about the game."

Willy shrugged. "We didn't have enough good players."

"Next year we'll win for sure," Sean added, lowering his eyes to the foot of the bed. "We'll have everybody back by then."

"Who played in goal?" Lizzie wondered aloud.

"Me." Sean shoved his hands in his pockets as he looked up. "But I couldn't play so good. Not like you." His face was beet red. "Trevor was supposed to play; after all, he was the backup, but he couldn't and so . . ."

"Trevor was very upset by the accident," Coach Powers cut in, his eyes suddenly cold and hard, and his jaw tightened as if he were holding something back. "Trevor said something about a dare . . . He didn't think Alex would go through with it. Anyway, he couldn't bring himself to play."

Willy took a step closer to the head of the bed and pulled a small, brightly wrapped gift from his pocket. He put it on Lizzie's lap. "The guys want you to have this."

Lizzie took her time untying the ribbon and removing the shiny paper, dragging out each exciting minute. Inside the box was a hockey puck. Also, under the tissue paper, was a small white card with the words: *Game puck from the finals.*

She was still holding the puck when she fell asleep that night.

The next morning, after she'd had her medication and was given a long list of instructions, Lizzie was discharged from the hospital. Although she could manage with her crutches just fine, she left the room in a wheelchair, as was hospital policy, and then her mother drove her to see Alex at another hospital.

Remembering Alex's fall, Lizzie was certain she'd fine him in terrible condition. Would he be covered from head to toe with a cast? Would Alex still look like Alex or some stranger in the bed? Since she'd never seen anyone who had been in a bad accident before, she prayed she wouldn't throw up or run from the room the minute she saw Alex. By the time she'd hobbled with crutches off the elevator at Alex's floor, her stomach was in knots.

While she and her mother were heading to the nurse's desk to ask for directions to Alex's room, a small, dark-haired woman approached them. "Lizzie?"

Lizzie recognized Alex's mother, a regular at the Tigers' games, and nodded.

"Hi, Mrs. Fabiano," Lizzie's mother said, reaching for the smaller woman's hand.

"Call me Linda, please."

"And I'm Laura."

Alex's mother smiled weakly. With eyes red and swollen, she looked like she'd been crying for days. In her hand was a paper cup half full of black coffee. "Would you like a hot drink before you go in to see Alex? I'd like to talk first."

"Sounds like a good idea to me," Laura said, eyeing a vending machine in the small lounge on the floor. Laura got two cups of hot chocolate, handed one to Lizzie, and then they sat on the couch across from Linda Fabiano.

"How's Alex?" Laura murmured.

Linda opened her mouth, but no words came out. Instead, she burst into deep sobs which shook her small body. Laura jumped up and wrapped her arms around Linda.

Lizzie held her breath. "What's wrong? Is it Alex? Is he worse?"

Linda sniffed and shook her head. "No, I'm sorry I scared you. He's actually shown a little improvement. It's just that . . ." Covering her face with her hands, she burst into sops again.

Smiling sympathetically, Laura turned to her daughter. "I think that Mrs. Fabiano is just relieved, now that the crisis is over. Sometimes the horror of an accident doesn't hit you until much later."

"Oh," Lizzie sighed.

"That's right." Linda looked up, her voice shaky. "I couldn't let go in front of Alex. I had to stay strong."

"I'm the same way," Laura said. "I held it together when we took Lizzie to the hospital and through all her tests and everything. Then I was a mess when I saw Pete, my fiancé, and I must have cried all over him."

"Fiancé? Does that mean that the wedding's back on?" Lizzie piped up.

"Yes." Laura's eyes brightened. "But now is not the time to talk about it. Later. Okay?"

Linda dabbed her eyes with a balled-up tissue, then glanced up. "I'm happy for you, Laura, and Lizzie, I want to thank you for what you did for Alex. You saved his life and I'll always be so grateful to you." She sprang from her seat and hugged her.

Lizzie winced, her arm still tender from the fall in the tunnel.

Linda stepped back. "I'm so sorry, Lizzie. I hurt you. How's the leg?"

"Itchy from the cast. But the pain's going away."

"The doctor says she's in pretty good shape, considering," Laura said.

"Well, the doctors are surprised about Alex, too," Linda said, casting her eyes down the hall. "Everybody is." She took a step to the coffee table and picked up a newspaper. "Look at this, Lizzie, you and Alex are in all the papers. You're a hero. And Alex, well . . . he's a miracle."

Lizzie studied the front page of the paper. The large, bold headlines seemed to scream the story. There were articles on the accident, the rescue and doctors' reports; there were quotes from Coach Powers about the Tigers' trip to the hockey tournament and how the players felt so bad about the accident that they

DAREDEVILS

didn't want to play in the final game. There was nothing about the *Double Dare Game*, though, just that Alex had been trying to walk on the cement base along the gorge and had fallen over the railing.

Lizzie assumed that Trevor, afraid of getting into trouble, had kept his big mouth shut about the accident. He'd told no one, except his team. He'd told the coach that he was so upset by Alex's fall that he couldn't play in the final game, and Lizzie wondered if Trevor was losing his mean streak.

On the second page of the paper was a copy of her team picture, taken just after the final game of the season last year. She was sitting in the front row in full gear with Willy on one side and Sean on the other, and she was scowling. Sean had made a big fuss on Picture Day just because he had to sit beside her on the bench. Since then, things had changed between them, Lizzie mused, smiling to herself. She handed the paper to her mother.

"Keep that paper, Laura," Linda said. "It's pretty special. Now, before we go into Alex's room, I thought I'd better prepare you. He looks pretty gruesome. You'll see a lot of bruising and swelling and cuts. His jaw was broken and his front teeth were knocked out." She let out a deep breath. "Apparently, he fell headfirst into the gorge, hit his face on rock and the impact turned him around. That's how he landed on his feet. He must have blacked out. The paramedics found him unconscious on the ledge."

They headed down the hall.

"Thank God there were no major head injuries," Laura said.

"Amazing, isn't it?" Linda's red eyes were wide. She slowly opened the door to Alex's room and lowered her voice. "Remember, he's in a lot better shape than he looks."

Lizzie limped on crutches into his room and stood beside the bed, her heart in her throat. Alex looked so little under the sheet and blankets, and he was so still. Wide strips of gauze, covering most of his face, were seeping with fresh blood in spots or black with dried blood in other spots. His purple and black eyes were swollen shut.

She sucked in a breath, fighting queasiness in the pit of her stomach. Alex was still Alex, she told herself, and her stomach began to settle.

He stirred, moaning, and he opened his eyes, which were two slits. They flickered recognition, then closed again. Lizzie gaped at her mother, wondering what to do next.

"He falls in and out of sleep like that," Linda Fabiano said. "He's getting better. I think he even recognized you."

Alex peeked through swollen lids again; then he slowly reached for Lizzie's hand.

CHAPTER 14

MASHED POTATOES AND GRAVY

"Trevor's gone," Emily told Lizzie as they were heading home from school through the slushy streets, with Lizzie on crutches, her cast covered with a plastic bag to keep it dry, and Emily toting the girls' bookbags.

"Huh?" Lizzie stopped dead in the middle of the sidewalk, not certain she'd heard right. "What's that?"

"Trevor's history at St. Mark's." Emily pushed back the glasses on her nose, while careful to keep the bookbags from sliding off her shoulders. "He's gone, thank God!"

Everybody knew that Coach Powers had kicked Trevor off the team not long after Alex's accident, but Lizzie thought she'd still see him around school. Thinking back, she realized that she hadn't heard Trevor's big mouth at St. Mark's for days. "Where did he go?"

"To St. John's and good riddance." Emily rolled her eyes.

The girls approached the intersection and waited for the lights to turn green. Emily shouted over the noisy cars whizzing past and the wind whistling through the trees. "At recess I overheard Sean telling Willy the whole story. Trevor's gone to live with his dad – who's separated from Trevor's mom – and since his dad lives near St. John, Trevor has had to go there."

"Tough luck for St. John." Lizzie made a face, and the girls burst out laughing.

"Sean says that Trevor's mom is making him live with his dad because Trevor needs a male influence," Emily went on. "But I think he's probably going there to get away from everybody here. The whole class is mad at him because of the accident. Nobody likes him, even Sean."

"That's right," Lizzie said, nodding. "Sean has been really nice to me lately, and everybody knows Trevor wouldn't like it one bit. Funny, the *old* Sean wouldn't dare get on Trevor's bad side."

"The *old* Sean was a big pain," Emily said.

The girls turned into the Lockyers' driveway. With Emily's help, Lizzie planted her crutches on the porch step and swung herself up, and then the girls made it though the front door and into the kitchen. Emily made hot chocolate with pink and green marshmallows on top and brought the mugs to the table. She didn't stay long. Lizzie and Laura had plans to go to a hockey banquet in North Lake that evening, and Lizzie had promised her mother that she'd rest beforehand.

In the family room, she took the wet plastic bag off her cast and propped her leg on the couch. There were signatures all over the cast. Instead of a dot, Nicole had drawn a small pink heart over the *i* in her name. In green magic marker, Tara had drawn the outline of a lizard, and inside the sketch, had scrawled the words: *Get better soon, Liz.* After Emily had searched the Internet for information on broken bones, saying it might come in handy one day when she was a doctor, she wrote on Lizzie's cast: *Great Work, Doc.* Lizzie especially liked what Willy had printed in black capital letters across the toe of her cast: *Number 1 Goalie.*

She stretched out on the couch and got lost in her thoughts about all the fuss made over her when she'd returned home after the accident. Her mother had brought her a pile of videos to watch and had allowed the television to be on all day for a solid week. Pete had bought her a book about the Leafs, and she'd read every word. Tara had stayed home from school to wait on her hand and foot, bringing her tea and toast and banana milkshakes whenever Lizzie so much as made a peep that she'd wanted something, and Tara hadn't complained a bit. She was eager to help – and not just because she got to stay home from school too. It was strange.

There had been a special assembly at school to honour her and Alex. Mr. Porcellato, the principal, had stood on the stage in the school auditorium and had said a bunch of nice things about Lizzie, calling her a hero in front of everybody. Ms. Borlino had given her a *Terrific Kid* certificate, which had all the signatures of the kids from her class on it. In the halls, she'd been stopped a hundred times by kids dying to hear about Niagara Falls, Alex's fall and the rescue, as well as all the gory details; Lizzie had loved telling the story again and again, adding more details with each telling, until mouths dropped open and eyes popped out. Her hockey team picture had been stapled on the bulletin board in the office and had been published in the school newsletter, along with a lengthy story about the accident, written by one of the teachers. Even Mrs. Salibo, the meanest teacher in the entire school, who hadn't cracked a smile in a million years, especially at a kid, had stopped Lizzie in the hall to say that she was proud of her. It was strange.

Alex couldn't attend the assembly because he was still in the hospital and would be there for many weeks, according to his doctors. With his jaw broken and his front teeth missing, he still couldn't talk or eat much. His eyes, however, were no longer black and blue and the swelling had gone down. Laura had phoned Linda Fabiano almost every day to find out about Alex's progress, and Lizzie had visited him several times; they'd played cards and electronic games for hours and hours.

DAREDEVILS

Lizzie glanced at the clock on the wall. It was almost time for her mother to come home. They were going to the North Lake arena, where the Hawks would be hosting the year-end banquet for the teams from the Niagara Falls tournament. She pushed herself up off the couch and hopped on her good foot to the stairs to get ready.

The blue dress hung in her bedroom closet. She took it off the hanger and held it against herself in the mirror, its shimmering material flowing to her ankles. It matched her eyes, as blue as a cloudless sky. Balancing on crutches while holding her dress, she had no hands to fix her hair. She imagined her long blonde hair swept off her neck; she'd look older, like a teenager.

Although normally she wouldn't be caught dead in a dress, she suddenly wanted to wear the blue dress to the banquet. She wouldn't dare, though, because her teammates would think she was weird. She hung the dress back in the closet and pulled out black pants and a white shirt to wear. The dress would stay on its hanger until her mother's wedding.

Joy Lynn Goddard

The wedding plans were all set. Laura and Pete were getting married in a few weeks, after Lizzie's cast was off and she could walk without hobbling down the aisle of the church as her mother's maid of honour. The ceremony would be simple, and the reception, at the house, would be small, with only a few friends and family members in attendance. Emily would be there, and Alex, if he were well enough by that time to attend, and Tara, of course, would be there, her carrot hair contrasting sharply with the red carnations in the living room. Tara, funky hair and all, wasn't so bad anymore, Lizzie realized, surprised.

The banquet hall was just the way Lizzie had dreamed it would be: round tables were draped with white linen tablecloths, a vase with a single red carnation at each one; the four teams from the Niagara Falls tournament were sitting with their families and friends around tables throughout the large room, and everybody was talking, laughing and having a good time.

Pete and Tara followed Laura and Lizzie to a table at the front of the hall to sit near the Northview Tigers. Speeches and an awards presentation would follow dinner. As the aroma of roast beef and gravy drifted throughout the room, Lizzie's stomach grumbled. Usually she couldn't eat a bite at the year-end banquet, with hopes of winning an award and her stomach doing flip-flops. But this year she might ask for second helpings. Her chances of winning an award, especially a top award, were next to nothing since she hadn't played in the final game, and this automatically disqualified her from winning.

She drowned her mashed potatoes in rich, hot gravy and picked up a fork. Tara was still playing with her food, swirling mounds of potatoes into high peaks in the middle of her plate, by the time Lizzie had finished her last bite.

Next, waiters carrying silver trays with lemon meringue pie and tall glasses of root beer, Lizzie's favourite drink, wove between the tables. As a waiter placed a slice of pie in front of Lizzie, Tara eyeballed

Joy Lynn Goddard

her. "You know, you may as well apply that pie directly to your hips."

Pete shot his daughter a dirty look.

"Oops." Tara smirked. "Just trying to be helpful."

Laura smiled at Pete and he kissed her hand, his eyes drawn to hers, as if nobody else were in the room.

"Gross," Tara groaned, rolling her eyes.

"Yuck," Lizzie made a face, and the girls burst out laughing.

When the microphone on stage crackled, all attention turned to the front of the room. One by one, the coaches got up to talk about the season. Coach Powers said that the Tigers had had the best season ever, despite losing the championship game. His players were strong and aggressive, like tigers, and had played well as a team. They'd lost the trophy in the final game, and Lizzie had pangs of regret.

When the coaches had finished discussing the season, the team awards were announced. Players received awards for sportsmanship and most improved player, for most valuable player and best defensive player. The tournament awards were given next.

Lost in her own thoughts, Lizzie was stunned when all eyes turned in her direction and applause thundered throughout the hall, echoing off the walls. Looking around, she wondered what all the commotion was about. Across the table, Laura gestured like a crazy woman towards the stage, then cupping her hands around her mouth, she shouted, "You won, Lizzie! Go get your award."

Lizzie's jaw dropped. She'd won something, but she didn't know what; she swung around to face the stage, hoping to find an answer.

At the microphone, Coach Powers beamed at her. "Looks like I need to repeat this announcement. This tournament's Most Valuable Goalie is Lizzie Lockyer. Come up here, Lizzie. The trophy's yours!"

With Pete's help, she made her way slowly to the stage, her crutches clunking across the hardwood floor. The coach helped her up the steps and across the stage, and then he took the microphone.

"You're shocked, Lizzie?" He raised an eyebrow.

She nodded, and there was laughter.

He turned to the crowd. "As you're all aware, Lizzie didn't play in the final game, and that would normally disqualify her from winning the Most Valuable Goalie award. But in speaking with the coaches and many of the players, we're all in agreement that Lizzie should win the award this year anyway."

There was dead silence in the hall. Not even the sound of shuffling feet, a cough or the clink of glasses could be heard as everyone waited for the coach to continue.

He put a hand on her shoulder. "The Tigers feel that they lost the final game because they didn't have their star goalie, Lizzie, who happened to be in the hospital when they played. With her, they had been on a winning streak. That's proof of her value."

When the crowd started to clap, Coach Powers held up his hand to silence them. "There's more. Lizzie showed herself to be a team player, something all coaches want from their players. She'd do anything for a teammate, including risk her life. She saved Alex, and that's the most valuable play this season. So the award's yours, Lizzie." He picked up the trophy from a table and handed it to her with a grin. "Congratulations!"

The Tigers were first to jump out of their seats and make a huge fuss over her. Clapping, shouting and stamping their feet, the sound was deafening. Soon everybody in the room was standing and cheering for Lizzie.

Coach Powers twisted the microphone in her direction. Bewildered by all the attention, she couldn't think of much to say, but it didn't matter because her words would have been lost in the noisy room anyway. Her face hot, and probably as red as the carnation in the vase at each table, Lizzie cleared her throat. "Thanks, um, Tigers . . . I never thought I'd . . ." Her voice trailed off with another round of applause.

She fixed her eyes on the trophy. It was hard to hold it while balancing crutches, but she'd never drop it or let anything happen to it. The trophy was too special. Tall, it had a wooden base with a silver-plated goalie on top, stick-ready. Engraved just under the goalie's skates was her name.

As soon as she got home, she'd clear a spot for her award on the white shelf above the desk in her room. She'd place it between the small plaque that she had won on Track and Field Day and the framed newspaper pictures of the Tigers. Just under the light, the trophy would catch her eye, and she'd look at it again and again and remember this moment.

The End

ABOUT THE AUTHOR

Joy Lynn Goddard has brought her vast experience in the classroom to her first children's novel, *Daredevils*. Her characters are composites of the many students she has taught – from the "weird" to the "brain" to the "jock." You'll love Lizzie, the feisty main character who dreams of finding her place on a boys' hockey team, and Alex, a teammate who helps plot against Lizzie's enemies. And you'll hate Trevor, Lizzie's nemesis, whose *Double Dare Game* leads Alex to the brink of the Niagara Gorge . . .

Even the reluctant reader will enjoy this book.

Joy Lynn Goddard shares her writing talents in the classroom and in the community. A former news reporter, she now works as a freelance writer and has had many articles and short stories published.

Printed in the United States
1063900002B/1-81